SECOND BEACH

A LIGHT-HEARTED ADVENTURE, AND A
SHORT STORY FOR ADULTS

PETER RIMMER

ABOUT PETER RIMMER

~

Peter Rimmer was born in London, England, and grew up in the south of the city where he went to school. After the Second World War, and aged eighteen, he joined the Royal Air Force, reaching the rank of Pilot Officer before he was nineteen. At the end of his National Service, he sailed for Africa to grow tobacco in what was then Rhodesia, now Zimbabwe.

The years went by and Peter found himself in Johannesburg where he established an insurance brokering company. Over 2% of the companies listed on the Johannesburg Stock Exchange were clients of Rimmer Associates. He opened branches in the United States of America, Australia and Hong Kong and travelled extensively between them.

Having lived a reclusive life on his beloved smallholding in Knysna, South Africa, for over 25 years, Peter passed away in July 2018. He has left an enormous legacy of unpublished work for his family to release over the coming years, and not only them but also his readers from around the world will sorely miss him. Peter Rimmer was 81 years old.

ALSO BY PETER RIMMER

❧

STANDALONE NOVELS

All Our Yesterdays

Cry of the Fish Eagle

Just the Memory of Love

Vultures in the Wind

❧

NOVELLA

Second Beach

❧

THE ASIAN SAGAS

Bend with the Wind (Book 1)

Each to His Own (Book 2)

❧

THE BRIGANDSHAW CHRONICLES

(*The Rise and Fall of the Anglo Saxon Empire*)

Echoes from the Past (Book 1)

Elephant Walk (Book 2)

Mad Dogs and Englishmen (Book 3)

To the Manor Born (Book 4)

On the Brink of Tears (Book 5)

Treason If You Lose (Book 6)

Horns of Dilemma (Book 7)

Lady Come Home (Book 8)

The Best of Times (Book 9)

THE PIONEERS

Morgandale (Book 1)

Carregan's Catch (Book 2)

First published in Great Britain in December 2018 by

KAMBA PUBLISHING, United Kingdom

10 9 8 7 6 5 4 3 2 1

Cover Design by *Toby Farrell, Kamba Publishing*

PROLOGUE — 1990

*P*ort St Johns was decked out in flags and bunting from the Cape Hermes Hotel to the Vuya Restaurant eight kilometres up the coast at Second Beach where it had all begun four years earlier when Hank was fourteen, going on fifteen, the same age as his friend Nteli, and Justine nearly seventeen.

The town was out to celebrate a twenty-first birthday for the star that was born on Second Beach; the happiness she was giving to everyone by coming back shone on their faces and she felt the excitement in the hugs she received when she ducked out of the helicopter with Strider. Nteli and the gang were in front, all but Nteli wearing school uniforms, Nteli having passed his examinations to enter the University of the Transkei. He had crammed into four years what took most kids twelve and some of his thanks went to Hank who had taught him English.

Justine looked for Mac over the heads of the crowd and her stomach still gave a lurch as she caught sight of the beard, the long hair and the leather hat. He was conspicuously a good head and shoulders above Johnny the

Fisherman and the rest of the Second Beach residents. Even Martin was there, clear-eyed and without his black cape or his battered Underwood typewriter. The crowd in between Mac and Justine parted and the man's soft brown eyes smiled at her as they walked towards each other across the grass of the football field, Strider keeping a pace behind his fiancée.

"You didn't forget your friends," Mac told her.

"I never will. We go back a long way, Mac. You remember Strider?" the two men smiled at each other.

Strider, shaking Mac's hand firmly said, "*The Great Man* still has a contract for you."

"I'm a local actor. Just for fun. Buys the beers."

"You'd never leave this place would you?"

"Not if I can help it. You made her a star," Mac murmured, turning to the most beautiful woman he had ever seen.

"She made herself. Four hundred million gross for her last three pictures."

They were approached by a municipal policeman. "Mr McIntyre, the Mayor asks will you join him with Miss van Heerden and her fiancé in the Mayor's car?"

"The Mayor has a car in Port St Johns?" wondered Mac in surprise.

"Has borrowed one for the occasion."

"I'd be delighted," and the crowd moved off across the field, Justine giving Johnny a hug, and then Fix Jalobe the local magistrate. Some of the black kids were singing and dancing but best of all, everyone was happy.

They drove straight to Second Beach, the entourage stretching forty cars down the road, half of them filled with newspaper reporters and cameramen from all over the world. They spilt out into the car park of the Vuya

Restaurant where the new owners had kindly lent the restaurant to Hector and Ricky for three days and the grin Hector gave Justine was for old friends. Behind them stood Hank, now tall, and Justine's mother and father.

Hank struck up with 'happy birthday' and the whole of Second Beach sang for Justine. After a hefty three cheers orchestrated by Mac, Hank, Nteli and the gang mingled among the guests offering ice-cold glasses of sparkling wine from the Cape. Through the tall milkwood trees, the beach was pure white and the great breakers of the Wild Coast rolled into the shore.

"What's this?" asked Strider as his future wife gave him a fifty-dollar bill.

Justine smiled up at her man. "Open it up. Look at the top right-hand corner."

"It's got my old telephone number."

"Don't you remember, darling?"

"Now I do... You've kept it all this time!"

"You told me to use the fifty dollars and phone you when I turned twenty-one."

Strider looked out over the beach to the wreck of the old German raider *Bremen* and he did remember, and the memories were sweet.

1

*M*ac had walked up the coast from Cape Town to Port St Johns with a light pack and the clothes on his back, a distance of one thousand four hundred kilometres. He was then in his thirties, lean, tall, burnt mahogany by the sun and free from the burdens of city life. Finding an old shed at the back of a new friend's garden, he had moved in, patching the leaking roof and making a seven-foot cot for his long frame out of driftwood and an old piece of foam rubber he scrounged in town from a lady whose cat had been stuck up her avocado tree. Mac had walked back the eight kilometres to Second Beach from Port St Johns with the foam rubber and a small sack of avocados and the promise of a kitten. What he was going to feed the cat on when he could not feed himself was the problem, so with an old piece of netting washed up on the shore, and weighed with pebbles, he made himself a throwing net and went after the mullet in the smooth-topped waters of the lagoon. It took him weeks of practice to catch just one of them.

By the time the kitten arrived and became a well-fed

tomcat, the shed had extended into a lounge with a separate bedroom. Outside under a spreading stinkwood tree was a braai and a hammock. A friend gave him a pair of bantams that took to living in the tree and every second day the hen laid him an egg for his breakfast. Out at the back, with seed given to him by another new friend, he planted a herb and vegetable garden and Mac settled down to live in the sun with his tomcat, two bantams, fish from the river, oysters, mussels and crayfish from the sea, friends in the village and friends in the small colony at Second Beach. There was a constant flow of holiday-makers too who came briefly to enjoy his lifestyle beneath the flowing boughs of the white stinkwood tree on the banks of the gentle lagoon, five hundred metres from the Wild Coast surf. His joy was the cry of the gulls in the morning, the calls of the hadeda, the chatter of the vervet monkeys, the dog-like barking of the dassies at night and the song of a thousand birds. He was the happiest man in the world.

JOHNNY HAD COME to Second Beach a refugee badgered for years by a wife: she always wanted him to make more money. When after five years she had given up and gone off with his best friend, Johnny had hitched his ski boat to his Land Rover and set out for the Wild Coast to go fishing. Johnny lived in one of the old cottages perched high on the hill overlooking the lagoon where Mac hunted the mullet for man and cat. Sometimes, when Johnny's charter party caught a big black steenbras or a gap-toothed musselcracker, they would feed him a beer in the Hermes bar and hear the tale of his earlier life. The story of his harassing wife varied according to his intake of beer but one thing was always the same: Johnny missed his best friend.

. . .

HAVING LEFT Durban because the *pot* he smoked was too expensive, Martin made his appearance in Second Beach. Making a living by carving story pictures on wide leather belts he had moved into a fallen down cottage, propped up enough of it to crawl inside and proceeded to blow out the rest of his brains by smoking the weed. The madness had crept into his life slowly but surely, puff by puff, and the hope of a great play he had come to write receded to nothing. Every morning though with a black opera cape thrown over his shoulders, he rushed up the hill with his portable Underwood and typed furiously under the hippo fig tree, ripping sheets from the roller and screaming his genius at the monkeys before rushing back down the hill at lunchtime, black cape streaming behind, and shouting, "I've got it, I've got it", the bunched up sheets of useless paper clutched in his fist. Mac fed him most of the time. There was no going back from the drug, Mac found. The man's brain, after twenty-five years of smoking marijuana, was almost destroyed.

NTELI LIVED under the wild mango tree outside the Second Beach holiday resort. With him were eleven friends and he was the leader of the gang. Nteli caught more crayfish, kicked a faster football and punched harder than anyone else. He was a very successful young man and could imagine no better way of going about his young life. He was fourteen, the same age as Hank who had taught him his rudimentary English in exchange for Hank's rudimentary Xhosa. Hank lived in Johannesburg so they only met once a year when Hank and the family came down to the coast on holiday.

Nteli was going to progress from catching crayfish on the

end of a piece of string that hung in the sea from the end of a bamboo pole with a limpet tied neatly to the end. He was going to be a gillie, get his own deep-sea fishing rod and get rich. Meanwhile, he slept on a piece of old cardboard round the driftwood fire and played football all day long on the beach. He owned a pair of shorts and an old shirt he washed once a week in the lagoon but had no shoes. He lived off tourists in the season by selling them his crayfish but out of school holidays his diet came mainly from the sea. Sometimes he could swipe a pawpaw but the pawpaw trees were closely watched by their owners. His biggest problem was keeping warm at night as the heat from the fire only warmed one side of his body when he was curled asleep on his piece of cardboard. The trick was for all the other kids to huddle up together taking turns to freeze on the perimeter. His mother and father were somewhere in the Transkei but he had lost touch with them when he was seven years old. Nteli's family was his gang.

THE LEOPARD KNEW MAC, Johnny, Martin and Nteli by sight though she kept well away from them. The coastal forest had shrunk to a few square kilometres of wild banana trees, the beak-nosed strelitzia of the Wild Coast, and was only rich and thick along the banks of the river and around the lagoon. The leopard slept in the hippo fig tree every day, the thick gnarled and twisted limbs giving her full protection from the antics of Mad Martin. She lived on dassies, had been tempted by the pigs that rooted deep in the forest, and had watched the herded cows and goats with relish. But nature's instinct for survival warned her against anything owned by man. The leopard's only problem was she left a telltale spore which Mac had picked up the day she moved into the forest. Every time Mac foraged in the forest, he looked for the leopard.

Overlooking the beach and lagoon from its perch, a little way up in the trees, was a beautiful thatched house that had seen better years; a hole in the veranda-thatch gaped at the sky and rats played merrily in the roof. Nobody had lived in the house for years and it was about to fall down when Aldo Carli made his first appearance. No one saw from where he came. He just arrived on a Tuesday morning with a two-year-old Land Cruiser and a smart ski boat. The first thing he did was cut Johnny's daily charter rate, and the second was to put up fancy posters in the holiday resort, on the municipal board at the Vuya Restaurant and at three points in Port St Johns itself. The attraction was the picture of Aldo Carli with satisfied customers standing next to a catch of seven black steenbras, four musselcrackers and a quantity of yellow bellies and seventy-fours. Aldo Carli had come to make his fortune and he made no bones about it.

First, he took a lease on the thatched house from the absentee owner and had the thatch renewed, the rats chased out and a good coat of paint put on everything. Cane furniture came down from Umtata and the man was free with his beers and proceeded to buy his friendships. Mac was tempted and even Mad Martin appeared under the new thatch on the veranda but there was something brash about the man that nobody liked.

Mac rationalised that if a man was good enough to dispense free food and beer who was he to criticise. He even got Johnny to go along on the principle that if you can't beat them join them. What they did not know was that Aldo Carli was after much bigger fish than the ones that swam in the sea and his ski boat operation was put together as the perfect front. The man was a crook.

HANK AND JUSTINE lived in Johannesburg with their parents and every year went on holiday to the Second Beach Holiday Resort. Justine was sixteen, going on seventeen and had fallen in love with Mac when she was fourteen years old. She was just waiting to grow up properly, leave school and return to Second Beach full-time as a latter-day hippie. She liked headbands, beaded bikinis, painting pictures and Mac. There was one snag. Mac had yet to realise she existed as a woman so that when the family drove in to the holiday resort, Justine had a big task on her hands. She was just short of five feet eight, gangly like a colt but all the bits were in the right places.

HECTOR WAS an eccentric who received a monthly cheque from the family trust and owned the Vuya Restaurant on lease from the municipality of Port St Johns. His partner, Ricky, was a Filipino, and they lived in the same house behind the best restaurant in the Cape where the food was nothing short of marvellous. They were known by one and all in Port St Johns as Rector and Hicky and the locals' trick when ordering food was to try to get the names right to their faces as otherwise, they were liable to too much pepper in the soup. Rumour had it that Hector had run away from his family at an early age to join the circus and had toured the world as a trapeze catcher but there were stories abroad about everyone in Port St Johns and no one took very much notice. There was even a rumour that Mac had stood for

Parliament in Cape Town but no one was able to conjure up a picture of Mac in a suit.

THROUGH THE TALL TREES, the Vuya gave a view of the foam-flung Wild Coast with the breakers streaming into shore from half a mile out to sea. Hector's other predilection was animals of which there were seven dogs, two cats and a gaggle of geese that came up from the lagoon every afternoon at four o'clock to be fed. Mac, when the sea was rough, the river mullet particularly crafty and his stomach grumbling, would have to look at the geese from the other side of the small lagoon. It seemed such a short distance to cross over the bridge but never did the geese, all seven of them, do so. They swam in the lagoon, even on Mac's side but they never stepped out on his shore.

2

On the day Justine and Hank arrived for their holiday, Mac had just about run out of food and he had a guest staying with him at the cottage, a man also prone to living off the land. The previous night Ricky had thrown his monthly tantrum and run off to his sister in East London taking Hector's new Land Cruiser and when Mac had asked after Ricky, Hector had thrown his own version of a tantrum slapping Mac's face, causing him to burst out laughing. Artists, even culinary artists, are temperamental.

So Mac had laid a trail of mealie pips from under the mango tree, across the bridge, through the trees, up the path to his cottage, across the stoep, through the rustic lounge and into the original shed that served as a kitchen; the last fifty pips had been soaked in Mac's home-brewed spirit (the still, deep in the forest away from all prying eyes). Mac and his houseguest had waited two hours and were just as surprised as the cat. The old gander came gobbling up the path, over the stoep, into the lounge and through to the kitchen where it ate the last pip that had been attached to a length of fishing line. The gander, now attached to the fishing line, which in its turn was attached to the kitchen door, obligingly pulled shut the door.

Finding itself trapped, the gander went berserk, cackling and hissing and cavorting from one side of the rustic kitchen to the other. Unbeknown, Justine in a sexy white pair of jeans and a powder blue boob tube, had followed in the wake of the gander with her brother to visit Mac, her infatuation, when the commotion was reaching its peak. Mac and his friend were in fits of laughter and the cat was sitting on the roof.

"What the hell?" cried Hank who was a young man of action at which Mac managed to control his laughter long enough to say, "Shush."

Justine struck a pose that was totally lost on Mac and the cat arched its back on the roof; slowly the cavorting in the kitchen subsided as the raw spirit did its work. Gingerly, Mac opened the kitchen door and peered inside at the gander fast asleep on the floor.

"It's dead," ventured Justine who had followed him into the kitchen, a kitchen now covered in gander feathers and down.

"Not really," said Mac. "Drunk but not dead."

"Are you going to eat that bird?"

"Not anymore. If a bird can make me laugh that much it deserves to live." Mac was still wiping the tears from his eyes.

"Bless my soul," gasped the friend who had bent down to inspect the gander. "The poor thing died from the alcohol or choked on the fishing line. This bird is dead."

Mac got down with his friend, "Oh dear, oh dear."

"What are we going to say to Hector?"

"Poor Hector. I'll think of something."

A mite miffed at not being the centre of attention,

Justine asked, "Daddy says will you come over for supper some time?"

Mac stood to his full height of six feet six inches and looked at Justine for the first time. "Either a feast or a famine... One year makes a difference," he said turning to Hank putting out his hand, "and how's my favourite young man?"

"I'm fine, thank you but what are you going to do with the goose? You going to give it back to Hector, Mac?"

"Somehow that doesn't seem right since the poor thing died in my kitchen. There's a trespass law on that one. How about we rig up a spit and roast the bird in style? A splendid bird like that deserves a splendid cooking."

THERE ARE moments in life when keeping a straight face is the most difficult thing on earth. Johnny, who had gone to the Vuya Restaurant later that morning to sell Hector fish found himself in just such a spot. He had chosen his moment wrong as it was feeding time for the geese and Hector had scattered bread on the lawn and was inspecting his flock when he realised something was altogether amiss.

"My gander's gone," he said softly in frozen horror. "My gander's gone!" he shrieked.

Some people love their birds more than people, and Johnny knew the restaurant owner to be one of those, and anyway he wanted to sell his fish, as he would want a beer later that day. Suppressing the convulsive lurch of mirth that welled up from his stomach he dutifully counted the squabbling geese and agreed with Hector, "There's one missing."

Down in front under the trees, Justine and Hank, an ice cold Coke apiece, were in fits of laughter: fortunately, they were hidden from Hector by the trunk of a tree and the noise of their laughter was swept away by ten cackling geese alarmed by Hector's outburst.

"Someone cook your goose?" Johnny let slip when the geese returned to eating their bread which sent Justine and Hank into further convulsions.

"It's not funny?" shouted Hector.

Johnny got down among the trees before the first surge of laughter began to choke him, "I'll come back later".

"And don't you laugh?" shouted Hector, stamping his feet on the pathway causing more pandemonium among the geese.

Johnny eventually calmed down, wiped the tears of mirth out of his eyes and saw Justine and Hank behind their tree.

"Hi, kids. You coming to Mac's braai tonight?"

"Can we come fishing tomorrow?"

"Seeing you two are my prize crew, what a question."

3

_____

 t the time Mac was placing the stuffed and trussed gander high over the open coals on a spit made of green wood from a wild fig tree, Aldo Carli was sitting on his stoep not far away, the new thatch shading his well-tanned body. Away in the distance at the far end of the beach on the rocks, he could see Justine sunbathing. Despite the relaxed and tropical atmosphere, the man was tense, his expression strained. Instead of picking up his binoculars to have a closer look at the bikini-clad Justine who looked a lot older than her sixteen years, he sat doing nothing but looking out to sea, waiting for the signal. Behind the thatched house was a tall mast that poked well above the house and surrounding trees, held rigid by strands of wire anchored to the ground.

When the bird was taking on a nice golden colour from Mac's careful basting and Justine and Hank were leaving the beach to change for Mac's braai, and dusk was less than an hour away, Aldo jumped as his sea-to-shore radio sprang to life with three, sharp emissions of static causing his tension to change to fear. They were coming for him. Rushing into the house, he knelt beside his transmitter and sent out his call sign in recognition. He then went to his cocktail cabinet and poured himself a large Cape brandy on the rocks. Aldo was not certain whether the drink was a pending celebration or a palliate for his nerves.

JUSTINE WORE the beaded headband and persuaded her mother that a little blue eyeshadow and lip gloss would be in order and again poured her body into the white jeans that left her shape in no doubt whatsoever. The blouse was a deep yellow, and she deliberately forgot to put on a bra, keeping her body from jiggling to deceive her mother who was only too well aware from the looks of the men and the boys that her daughter was now a young woman. Justine let her long blonde hair hang around her well-tanned shoulders.

Strolling out of the holiday resort, the family waved at Nteli and his friends who were separating the flesh from the small limpets they had cut from the rocks for bait. Hank had hung back.

"Where?"

"The rock-ship, when the moon comes up," whispered Nteli.

"I'll bring some goose for you all."

Dusk was settled on the enclave at Second Beach and when the family crossed the bridge, the fish were already plopping in the lagoon. Upon the hill to the left, all the lights were blazing in Aldo Carli's house, the generator thumping away. There was not a breath of wind and the air was cooling as the last of the sun flushed the hills behind Mac's cottage. As they walked through the dusk, they could smell the roasting goose.

. . .

MAD MARTIN HAD READ a poem in English and Afrikaans that was gibberish in both official languages and threw his black cape over his shoulders and left the braai with a flourish of artistic temperament. The bird had cooked to perfection, the thick outside fat reduced to a crunchy delight that Mac had basted with honey, white wine and herbs from his garden.

At ten o'clock when the moon came up above The Gap, Hank excused himself, purloined a good few slices of meat with Mac's encouragement and left the gander feast carrying his father's torch.

AT THE ROCK-SHIP, which projected far into the breakers, a geological freak the waves of a millennium had not eaten away, Hank joined Nteli and his gang and was given a fifteen feet bamboo pole, cut from a clump of bamboo found on Wella Panchwa's farm. A long line of string hung from the end of the pole ending in a limpet which he hung over the rock-ship down into the dark water of the sea. The hope was for a crayfish to be stupid enough to grip the limpet and in its greed, refuse to let go and allow itself to be pulled up, inch by inch out of the water into the hands of the waiting boy. Nine times out of ten, the crayfish fell back into the sea but it was a lot of fun. By midnight when Hank knew he should be finding his way home, they had seventeen crayfish.

"Did you see that, Nteli?" Hank spoke in Xhosa and pointed to the far horizon, across the moon-bathed sea to where a light was flashing.

"I see it twice now."

"That's Morse code," conveying nothing to Nteli or his friends.

"There are dots and dashes," Hank tried to explain. "People talk to each other in dots and dashes."

In Xhosa, the explanation sounded ridiculous and the boys all laughed politely at the white boy. Peeved they were not impressed with his knowledge, he tried in English but only Nteli understood.

"What are they saying, Hank?"

"Don't know. They've only taught me the SOS. That's the distress at sea call. I go to scouts second Wednesday every month."

"What are scouts?" and the two boys were off on another tangent in the way of explaining their totally different ways of life. Nteli was impressed by his friend and tried to explain the Morse code to his gang and received a gale of laughter for his trouble.

"Better go," said Hank. "Dad stays awake."

FIVE MINUTES LATER, Hank wound his way down the path onto the beach in front of the thatched house and was surprised to see two men launching a ski boat into the white phosphorescent surf, trying without success to break out of the rollers to the open sea. Hank watched for ten minutes until the ski boat landed back on the beach and was hauled out of the water by a waiting Land Cruiser. Hank was in the shadow from the moon and waited for the Land Cruiser and the boat to leave the beach before carrying on to the holiday resort. As hard as he tried, he could not see who was in the boat or driving the Land Cruiser but he knew for certain that it was not Johnny the Fisherman as it was not Johnny's boat or his Land Rover.

Puzzled, he let himself into the kombi tent and told his father why he was late.

"That's funny, Hank. Who'd ever want to go fishing at night in a heavy swell...? There's cocoa in the flask."

"Go to sleep you two," chided his mother from the far side of the tent. Justine was fast asleep, pursuing Mac in her dreams.

4

*I*n the early hours, the leopard came down and took away the carcass six metres away from where Mac was sleeping with his bedroom window wide open to the night.

HANK WAS up with the dawn. He and Johnny stood together under the trees at the top of the beach looking out at the rollers crashing into the shore.

"Big holes in the water," said Johnny after ten minutes.

"Big holes in the water," repeated Hank. It was the signal that fishing was off for the day: they would be unable to get the ski boat out through the surf without being capsized by the six-meter breakers. "Wild," declared Hank in awe of the sea. "That sea's wild, man."

"Maybe tomorrow. The winds changed five points to the east."

"They were trying to get out last night."

"Who were?"

"Couldn't see. I'd been fishing for crayfish with Nteli. Midnight. These men were trying to launch a ski boat. Why would anyone want to go fishing in the middle of the night, Johnny?"

"Beats me. Must be Aldo Carli. No one else has a boat on Second Beach."

"Pulled it up the beach with a Land Cruiser. I could see it was a Toyota Cruiser by the silhouette."

"That's him... There's something about that man that doesn't make sense... No one fishes these waters at night except in the river mouth down by First Beach. The Wild Coast is dangerous enough during the day. You sure he was trying to get out?"

"He was out by the fourth breaker where the rollers get big. Ran up and down for ten minutes looking for a gap."

"Better go and get Mac to take you netting for mullet. We aren't going fishing out there today."

DESPITE THE BIG SEA SWELL, the day was crystal calm, and the trees reflected perfectly in the lagoon, and a pied kingfisher perched on the power line that took electricity way up over the hills to Third Beach.

Out in the centre of the shallow lagoon, waist deep in cool clear water, Mac and Hank were wading slowly forward, Hank holding the net correctly and Mac tipping his finger ahead to show Hank where he had seen a shoal of mullet. Ever so slowly, they moved closer to the fish until Mac gave the signal and Hank flicked the net out, forcing the stones to keep the net taut in a circle landing above the fish and sinking over them. The stones around the edge dropped faster than the centre of the net, which pocketed around the fish, the long pocket of fish and net turning on its side as Hank pulled the drawstring.

"Gently, boy. Gently, boy. There you go. Gently, boy. Smoothly. Just smoothly. You've got them. They're in the net."

"Hey look at that Mac. There are seven fish and that one weighs all of half a kilo."

"We'll have them over the fire for breakfast."

"Your cat's going to like you."

"A leopard stole the carcass last night. There's spore all around my cottage."

"A leopard!"

"A big female cat. Seen her spore in the forest."

"Aren't they dangerous?"

"Not if people leave them alone. Been there for a long time and never touched the cattle. Plenty of dassies. Without that leopard, the place would be overrun by rock-rabbits."

"You've seen her?"

"Not even once."

"Wow! A leopard... These fish are really wriggly in the net."

WHILE HANK WAS MONOPOLISING MAC, Justine took herself off to the beach to improve her tan. Applying herself thoroughly with oil, she lay out on the same rock and soaked up the morning sun. At the top of the beach, a herd of cows stood motionless in the sun, their heads facing the slightly cool breeze that came in from the sea. All of them were chewing the cud and Justine chuckled at cows catching tans. Above, a black-backed gull had caught a thermal drifting high in the sky dipping and diving for the sheer joy of life. In front, the breakers crashed, and the sea rolled in, the sea a seething mass of pure white foam.

Aldo picked her up through his binoculars and went inside to put on his trunks and pick up a towel before going down to the beach.

"Hi, you on holiday?"

Justine opened her eyes and shaded them with her hand. A man was looking down at her from out of the sun.

"And you?" she nodded asking in return after registering a good-looking man.

"Live here. That's my house. One with the thatched roof. You alone?"

"Sure... My! Quite a house. The roof was almost off last year."

"Cost a fortune to repair. Want some coffee? A drink?"

"What time is it?"

"Eleven o'clock."

"What the hell. I'm on holiday. A drink would be fine."

"My name is Aldo. What's yours?"

"Justine."

"That's a lovely name for a lovely girl. Give me your towel. We can walk through the lagoon up to my house. The tide's in... I like that chain around your ankle."

"You do?"

"Chains around ankles are sexy. Ask any Italian."

FAR OUT TO SEA, the freighter slipped over the horizon where it anchored and waited, its Greek captain out of humour.

"Make it appear the engine's broken down," he shouted at his chief engineer.

"Don't blame me. It's the Wild Coast. You can't have everything skipper."

"You're right. Nothing is ever easy."

HAVING drunk the first vodka and coke of her life (it actually was a treble as Aldo had spiked her drink) Justine felt distinctly wobbly and excused herself to go to the bathroom.

"Last door on the right," said Aldo, taking in the effect of the drink and the length of Justine's legs: she was still wearing her bikini. "Not that one." Aldo had followed her into the house trying to decide whether the time was right to make his pass. Justine had opened the last door on the left and found it full of black rubbish bags stacked to the ceiling, each one neatly tied at the mouth and none of them showing any spillage.

Justine backed off and crossed the corridor to the bathroom. "Why do you keep so much rubbish in the house?"

"Just polystyrene. Buoyancy for the ski boats. We're getting two more ready to go to sea."

Justine found herself inside the bathroom, gratefully closed the door, ran to the pan and was promptly sick, moisture breaking out on her brow. Having removed the offending liquor from her stomach she quickly felt better and splashed water over her face and neck. "How does dad drink six of those in one evening?" she whispered to herself.

By the time she returned to the stoep, Aldo had locked the room where she had found the black bags.

"Thanks for the drink... You'd better do something about all that rubbish."

"It isn't rubbish," said Aldo passing her her towel. A man

of considerable experience knew when not to make a pass. "Come again."

Justine murmured, "Maybe," thinking through her next step in her plan to make Mac jealous. If it was the last thing she was going to do on her holiday, she was going to make Mac look at her as a woman; she was going to make Mac want her. Of the Italian, she was sure he wanted to kiss her.

5

$\mathcal{T}$he Greek radar operator saw the five blips move quickly across his screen in perfect formation and spoke to his captain.

"Military or police helicopters coming up the coast, captain. Perfect formation."

"You are sure they are military?"

"What else can they be?"

The captain spoke crisply to his first officer who had the anchor up and the ship underway before the five specks were visible in the captain's binoculars. Speaking into the tube to his coxswain, "East north east... Let's get out of here." Looking down from the bridge, the captain was pleased to see a wake build up under his bows as the vessel moved further out into international waters. "Send a one-night abort signal," he told his radio operator.

"Radar signal stationary on the screen," said the radar operator over the tube.

"How far from Port St Johns?"

"Thirty kilometres... Now moving up the coast again."

"Speed ten knots," they heard the coxswain's voice.

"Well, they are not after us. Take the bridge Mr Tselentis."

"Aye, aye sir."

THE HELICOPTERS LANDED TOGETHER on Second Beach sending the cows off at a run and bringing everything else to a standstill. Mac and Hank had finished their late breakfast, and the cat was eating what was left of the mullet. Justine sat up on her rock feeling better from a short nap. Aldo heard the abort signal and panicked, rushing to his Land Cruiser before realising the choppers could follow him anywhere. Mad Martin lit a joint to calm his nerves. With five sets of rotor blades screaming not a hundred metres from the restaurant, Hector and Ricky came out to see what all the fuss was about: people were flooding out of the helicopters onto the beach, crouching down from the air pressure of the blades.

The first man out, walked briskly across the sand, turned around once to have another look at everything and then walked between the trees up to Hector and Ricky and all seven dogs.

"Can we have lunch for seventy-six people?" inquired the man. He was wearing a bright green T-shirt with a picture of yellow palm trees and a girl in a red bikini. Hector was fascinated.

"Those colours clash you know?" he observed pointing at the shirt. "We don't have that many customers in the whole of Port St Johns and my restaurant seats thirty-six."

"Put some tables under those trees. Spill out onto the beach. We've been up and down the coast all morning. Name's Warnaby. Cannon films. We're going to make a movie." Warnaby put his hand out to Hector and Ricky in turn and both gave it a wet handshake. "This is Second Beach, Port St Johns?"

"That it is."

"Well? Can you do lunch?"

"Take a while Mr Honeybee." Hector usually got the names wrong.

"How long?"

"Two hours."

"Hour an' a half."

"Fish be all right?"

"Just fine. You've a reputation."

The panic was on.

A BOY from the kitchen was sent running down the beach to find Johnny the Fisherman who had fish to sell. The big oven was lit that could take a forty kilogram musselcracker whole. Another man was sent to plead with Mac for lettuce, carrots, celery and anything else that would go into a salad. Ricky rushed off into town in the Land Cruiser (his trip to East London had been predictably short-lived) to buy fresh rolls from the baker and bring back anything else that was edible. Hector went into a flat spin and forgot about the loss of his gander.

On the beach, the beautiful people were spilling out all over the place and everyone was very excited. The *in* word was *perfect* and everyone was using it at the same time. Justine, watching everything from her vantage point on the rocks thought she had never seen so many dishy men in all her life. A transit van had arrived with camping equipment being unloaded from it and taken to the municipal campsite that overlooked the beach, and there were more shouts of *perfect* carrying across the sand, the breakers having calmed down to a gentle stroll into the shore.

A bevy of bikini-clad girls burst down from the campsite for a swim in the warm water, all of them keeping their hair from getting wet. The helicopters took off again and flew down the coast growing smaller and smaller before flying away around the heads causing Aldo to get out of his Land Cruiser and stagger back into his house where he heard the third abort signal. Pouring himself a stiff brandy, all thoughts of making a pass at Justine was shaken out of his mind by a mixture of shattered nerves and relief.

Mac strolled up the beach carrying a sack of fresh vegetables from his garden, the long stride causing Hank beside him to take two steps to his one. Mac waved to Justine on her rock causing butterflies to fly around in her stomach: even with a beach full of gorgeous men, he was still the best-looking man in her life. The curved pipe was clamped in his mouth and his smile was warm and playful.

"You'd better come and help," he called to her. The three of them walked up to the restaurant and went around the back into the kitchen where Johnny was delivering a musselcracker that had taken up the entire space in his paraffin fridge.

"Brought some help," explained Mac smiling broadly and taking the pipe out of his mouth and putting it in his pocket; the pipe had gone out anyway.

"For the first time in my life, Mac, you are welcome in my kitchen," laughed Hector.

"Let's go then... get trestle tables under the trees... Justine, start helping the girls cut up the salads... Hank, I taught you how to open oysters last year. Remember the muscle to cut is at seven o'clock when the shell is pointing away from you... How long are they staying?"

"I don't want to even think about that," exclaimed Hector.

WHILST ORGANISED chaos prevailed in the kitchen at the Vuya Restaurant, Aldo made his plans. The two men who were staying with him to help rebuild the new boats were given an ultimatum.

"We have missed one night and will miss another. Our friends will wait till Thursday and after that, the opportunity to ship in bulk will be lost. We will be back to the problems of road transport and Transkei politics. Those boats must be finished. The moon is full tonight and then the sea will flatten. We will load tomorrow night before the moon rises. All three boats. I want those boats seaworthy. That film crew is our cover. Imagine how much they will need. On Thursday, we are going out to fish. We will unload and still have time to fish. Then we'll have a real party with all those birds I can see on the beach," and he passed his binoculars to his *friends* who ogled the ladies of the film crew one by one.

ONE HOUR and forty minutes after Peter Warnaby had placed his lunch order, the film crew were seated at long tables under the trees facing a table that was covered in trays of food with the musselcracker taking centre stage.

"Lunch is served," announced Hector from the steps. He then led his staff and helpers towards the food table. Earlier Justine and Hank had run back to the camp to change and found a 'gone fishing' sign on the kombi tent in their father's writing. Justine had scribbled a note in return as to where they could be found. She put on a Pondo bead skirt and hung a string of beads over her bikini top. With Hank changed, they had walked back to the restaurant.

"You wear this behind your ear," Mac said, fitting a hibiscus flower in her hair.

She followed the kitchen staff; Mac was wearing a monkey-skin over one shoulder, Johnny a flashy shirt he had bought on Durban beach and Hank in his three-quarter jeans and Wild Coast T-shirt. Hector was resplendent in a Filipino shirt he had collected along with Ricky in Manila. They served trays of open oysters that had been scattered with bougainvillaea petals; slithers of lemon from Mac's tree lay among the shells.

"I was thinking of ordering supper," Peter Warnaby said later in full appreciation.

"Don't you dare," mocked Hector.

"Who was the pretty blonde girl?"

"Tourist."

"I could use her as an extra, along with the tall man and the one with the Durban shirt. You think they'd mind?"

6

The male leopard took the scent and followed it downwind. He had left his pride in the hills above the south coast of Natal and walked down through the coastal forest taking to the hills for food and keeping well out of the way of man. He was a magnificent specimen in the prime of his life and he needed a mate. He cut the spore behind Mac's cottage and followed it up the hill, the offshore wind sending tantalising whiffs that made him want to purr with satisfaction. By the time he reached the vine-like hippo fig tree, the female had flattened herself, a prime instinct pulsing through her blood and causing the tip of her tail to flick. She heard the male cough from ten metres below as he walked around the base of the tree and her tail slashed and gave away her position. The male threw caution to the wind and launched himself upwards, a blur of yellow power. The male was ready to fight but the female leopard on the treetop rolled onto her back and purred, her golden eyes smiling at him as if she had known him all her life. She was a beautiful cat, and the male was well pleased with his journey.

. . .

THE GERMAN RAIDER *Bremen* had come ashore in 1914. A storm had hurled the ship onto the rocks below Nteli's fishing spot, which was why fishing for crayfish was so good as the rusted old hulk gave the crustaceans protection from the breaking waves. The main guns had long been removed along with any valuables but the silhouette was still of a proud ship going to war. With the evening sun behind the hulk, it was exactly what the film crew had searched for along the coast, checking out the known wrecks as they went.

"If the sea will let us have her long enough," Peter Warnaby told Mac, "We will have that old ship as good as new. The script says the ship came ashore last night, and with paint and special effects, she'll look just that to the camera. What do you think, Strider?"

"Depends on the sea," replied the American cameraman tugging at his right ear.

"Full moon tonight," added Mac. "You may have timed it nicely. The Wild Coast calms down after the full moon. Or it's meant to. How long do you need?"

"Three days. Just three days."

"Never trust the sea," Johnny told them. "This coast turns nasty in six hours. Who's coming to the bar?"

"Nothing we can do today. You coming young lady?" asked Strider turning to Justine. Behind him, Mac tried to open his mouth but shut it quickly when Justine shot him a look.

"Not for me," said Hank. "Enjoy yourself, sister dear," and he was off across the beach to join Nteli's gang in a game of football.

"Drinks are on us," smiled Strider, which were words of

great relief to Johnny who enjoyed his beers but never had enough money to pay for them. "Six spray guns can paint that hulk in a morning," went on Strider. "Grey paint for war."

Justine grinned sweetly at Mac and followed the men to Johnny's Land Rover.

"Why would Aldo store hundreds of rubbish bags in his house, Mac?" she wanted to know looking back to the thatched house halfway up the hill to the right of the *Bremen*.

"What?"

"Black bags. All full. He asked me up for a drink."

"Be careful of Aldo Carli."

"I know. He did make me feel uncomfortable."

Justine turned to follow the others across the beach but Mac stayed looking up at the thatched house. "So that's what he's up to?" he speculated under his breath. "You go on," he called. "Just remembered something," and Justine was torn between following Johnny and going after Mac who was walking purposefully towards the thatched house.

"Want a drink, Mac?"

"Not from you, Carli. Not content with ruining Johnny's business you want to have the police down on the colony. There are a lot of artists living comfortably doing their own thing. If you disturb our tranquillity, I'll break your neck."

"You threatening me?"

"Yes!"

"I don't know what you are talking about. Go, Mac. You're out of your depth."

"You going to force me?"

"No. But the two men behind you are." They had come

up from the boats and smiled at Mac when he turned to look at them; both were carrying steel pipes. He looked back at Aldo who was also smiling and left the stoep with Aldo's laughter ringing in his ears.

MAC SAT THINKING for some time watching his bantams pecking for food outside his cottage. The loincloth around his middle was the only concession to civilisation. The Italian had something important to hide was his conclusion but he could not see the point of a room full of contraband. There was no traffic to buy and sell anything as the colony was at the end of the road except for the track to Third Beach with its six huts for hikers. A man does not threaten to assault you unless there is a reason and Mac did not think the reason was Justine. They knew nothing about the man. He had arrived with his boat and said nothing, months later bringing in the other two they were repairing. Mac thought of his friend the magistrate and decided to ask Fix Jalobe to check him out. As a foreigner to Southern Africa, Aldo Carli would have needed a Transkei visa, and they only issued those two weeks at a time. Mac got up and strode around his cottage to take a walk in the forest and cut the male leopard's spore getting down on his haunches to have a better look. A fainter and smaller spore, dusted by the wind, was pressed into the earth next to the fresh print.

Smiling to himself, he said, "We've got ourselves a visitor," and began to follow the spore through the wild banana trees.

By the time Mac stood beside the vast girth of the hippo fig tree, the big cats had spread themselves on their sides in the sun and only an aeroplane would have seen their paws stretched out towards each other, centimetres apart. The big male had stretched his neck back and was rubbing his ear on the tree with satisfaction and the female was watching him with gentle pleasure. They had both heard the man down below but took no notice; they would hear him soon enough if he tried to climb the tree.

Mac looked at the fresh spore that stopped at the foot of the multi-trunked tree and stood back for a better look. Glancing around he found what he wanted and climbed to the top of the small stinkwood tree that barely supported his weight.

"Beautiful." Both cats were looking at him but neither bothered to move. Mac was not sure, but he thought the rhythmic rumble from the female was a purr and he climbed down his tree feeling better for seeing them. "Big cats fall in love just like anyone else," he told himself; it was that obvious.

7

*H*ank found a Cape Salmon hanging on the tree next to the family kombi and his father looking very pleased with himself.

"Down by First Beach at the river mouth. They go upriver to spawn at this time of the year. Thirty kilograms! Fought me all the way. Took half an hour to get the fish out of the water."

"Wow... What a fish," shrieked Hank walking around the monster. "Look at the size of the scales. How are we going to eat all that fish without a freezer?"

"I've the idea to throw a beach braai and invite all our friends. Make big fires. Get some mussels off the rocks and roast them. Johnny plays the guitar."

"Did you see the film crew? Justine's with Johnny talking to them."

"I know. Saw her go into the Hermes."

"You didn't stop her, dad?"

"She's nearly seventeen and looks older anyway. She's a sensible enough girl your sister and Johnny's a good friend."

"Can we get some Cokes for Nteli and his gang?"

. . .

THE IDEA WAS for Justine to go and talk to Aldo Carli and keep him busy and for Nteli and his friends to keep an eye on the other two at the boats, imitating an owl if either of the men went up to the thatched house. Meanwhile, Hank would go around the back and get into the house from the kitchen.

Aldo was surprised to see the girl back on his stoep. He had just sent a coded signal to the Greek freighter giving the time of delivery.

"You want to join us for a beach party?" she asked a little nervously. "Dad caught a fish."

"Sounds good to me."

"Come down and meet my folks."

"Your folks here?"

"Sure. How else do I go on holiday?"

"How old are you?"

"Eighteen," she lied and led him away from the house down the path through the shallow part of the lagoon and onto the beach.

TEN MINUTES later when the three driftwood fires were lit on the beach, Hank, Nteli and his gang joined the party.

"The door's locked," he whispered to his sister, "and there are burglar bars on the window."

"Could you see the black bags?"

"The curtains were drawn. Anyway, why did you invite him to the party, Justine?"

"What else could I do? Maybe we'll find out something."

. . .

THE STILL SURFACE of the lagoon mirrored the green trees and red poinsettias on the banks and the late sun bathed the beach in yellow, translucent light. The old wreck took on a newer look, and the fires burned brighter in the gloaming. The fish was brought down from the campsite, laid out and displayed on a table for everyone to have a good look at. The tide was right out and for the first time in days, the Wild Coast was at peace with itself. Up by the thatched house arc lights shone on the two boats under repair while the hadedas flew home to roost shrieking at each other and the bats came out to feast on the insects. A dog barked in the distance, the lonely sound lost in the evening.

Like all parties, it started slowly, people drifting from group to group, happy in the balm of the warm, tropical air that drifted the scent of jasmine down the hills from around the cottages. Hector sent over bowls of salad from the restaurant, a thank you for the help they had given him over lunch. Later, a closed sign appeared on the door of the Vuya and Hector and his staff drifted down to the beach with the dogs. Some of the film crew thought the party was laid on for them, and nobody minded, and the bonfires showed the groups of people as the light totally faded and the stars came out in the heavens. People drifted off and came back with wine and beers and one of the film people found a harmonica and began gently playing to the big moon that rose from the sea, an orange ball of dying fire. Up at the cottages, Mad Martin pulled the black cape over his shoulders, rushed up the hill with his Underwood and sat under the hippo fig tree bashing at the keys before rushing back to his cottage again. He was writing a nocturnal play in both official languages.

8

───────

*a*t ten o'clock the next day, the rays of the sun reached Johnny the Fisherman under his tree and woke him up to a monster *babalas*. He sat up and groaned at the pain, using the trunk of the tree to pull himself on to his feet.

"Never drink the dreaded red after beer," he mumbled trying to work out what he was doing under a tree; the dreaded red was Tassenberg red wine.

"Want a beer?" joked one of the film crew as he walked past to the wreck of the *Bremen*, now a hive of painters.

"Go away," hissed Johnny straining to bring his eyes into focus. The crash of the sea had given way to a perfect stillness, and the ocean was flat and sparkled with a million fish scales. He looked at the wild banana trees up on the hill behind the thatched house and the fronds were still and lifeless. Up in the sky it was a pure blue and the sun was hot. He studied the sea for a full ten minutes before making his decision.

. . .

FROM THE GARAGE of the thatched house Aldo Carli drove out in a black panel van, checked to look at the two ski boats nearing completion and drove away over the bridge passing Nteli and the ten remaining geese under a wild fig tree as he headed for the country. On his way from a swim, Mac saw him pass and wondered where he was going.

"What's he need two cars for anyway?" he asked himself, referring to the Land Cruiser and the black panel van that was going away from him down the road towards the restaurant.

HALF AN HOUR LATER, when Johnny was calling Hank and Justine out of bed to go fishing, the panel van called at the first village and two men came out of a hut carrying two black rubbish bags neatly tied at the top. Aldo Carli speaking in perfect Xhosa (he discarded his Italian identity when he left Port St Johns) paid the men two hundred rand in old notes and put the bags in the back of the van. Earlier in the year, he had called on the men and given them a special seed to plant in between the rows of their mealies. The two men went back into the hut well pleased with the transaction. The van drove off to the next village where the process continued.

JOHNNY USED the fish finder (sonar equipment that showed up anything solid underwater, fish included) to get over the reef and then threw the sea anchor overboard and the serious business of fishing was quickly underway. Two big hooks were baited for each rod, Johnny showing Justine and Hank how to tie on the pilchard and the squid with a twist of cotton that would stop the big fish sucking the food off the hooks. One by one, the rods went over the side and the lines ran down into the ocean, the lead sinkers pulling the lines taut. Justine held her index finger on the line and concentrated on differentiating between a fish knock and her sinker tapping the bottom. Johnny put out two lines for himself and cursed his red wine hangover; the boat rolled with the slight swell, doing nothing for his stomach.

"Must be engine trouble," he concluded nodding at the Greek freighter. "That ship was in the same place yesterday."

"How old is Mac?" asked Justine.

"He doesn't have an age," replied Johnny "... That was a knock. Any knocks, Hank?"

"A couple."

"There're fish down there."

"Has he ever been married?"

"Whoever would marry Mac and live in that shack?"

"I think his cottage is very romantic. Money isn't everything. Dad's always saying that."

"Usually when he's short," reminded Hank.

"I could easily live at Second Beach," mused Justine. Johnny gave her a queer look. "This is paradise. I'm never bored in Port St Johns... Why do they call it a port?"

"There used to be a jetty before a storm washed it out to sea and the river silted up. Before my time. Easy, Hank. You've got him. Just wind him up. That's the way. Hell, I've got one too."

"So have I," yelled Justine with fright. "What do I do! *What do I do!*"

"Wind him up and keep your line away from mine. Hey, hey! Wind Justine. Just wind!"

"Here comes mine," yelped Hank pulling his fish into the boat.

"Go and help your sister."

Squealing with excitement, Justine shouted, "It's so big! Leave me alone, Hank. Must be a shark. Look at the rod bending."

"Let out the line," Johnny told her, landing his own fish in the boat. "Let him run and then pull him in again. That's my girl. Yellow bellies," he explained looking at the fish in the bottom of the boat. "Don't let him snap your line, Justine," seeing the tension on it.

"Please help, Hank."

"You didn't want any."

"*Help me!*"

Hank got both his arms around his sister and his hands on the rod and felt the pull. "*Wow!* What is it, Johnny?"

"Wind him in."

The fish came up and took off into the air like a missile from a submarine, the huge wings still flapping from its fight to free the hook. Johnny dropped his rod and whipped his knife from its sheath and ran to cut the line.

"What was it?" breathed Justine as the monster fell back into the sea and vanished.

"A ray," said Johnny. "An electric ray. That fellow could have sunk the boat."

NINETY-SIX KILOMETRES away Aldo Carli called at an engineering works in Umtata and loaded the big steel trap into the panel van in front of the black bags and headed back for Port St Johns. The jaws of the trap were ugly and the springs that clamped them together the size of a man's fist. The Sangoma would be pleased, he told himself as it was always best to be on the right side of the witch doctor in rural Africa. The man to whom he was going to give the leopard for *muti* was more powerful than the Paramount Chief. Aldo Carli was greatly pleased with his purchase.

BY THREE O'CLOCK in the afternoon Second Beach and the cottages were a hive of industry. Mad Martin sat cross-legged on the grass outside his door cutting the pattern of a peacock into a six-inch-wide belt of leather. He was humming to himself having succumbed to the buzzing noises in his head to which he was composing words in English and Afrikaans. The tree giving him shade for his labour cascaded with a pale orange bougainvillaea and one of the petals fell onto his head and bobbed precariously to the music.

In the lagoon, Nteli and his gang were working at the art of playing and the shrill cries of treble voices tinkled through the trees as the game of splash and chase progressed through the warm water.

Mac was making himself a pair of leather boots from a piece of nicely tanned leather; he was at the tricky stage of tacking on the sole before stitching but his concentration was constantly being broken by a troop of monkeys playing hide and seek in the wild banana trees. On his day-bed outside on the stoep lay a replete cat whose tummy was as tight as a drum having eaten too much of the leftovers of the fish that Mac had salvaged from the beach braai.

Through the trees across to the right of the lagoon, the painting of the bow of the *Bremen* was complete, and a helicopter was landing on the beach with the blades still rotating. *The Great Man* stepped out of the chopper and the film was ready to roll: the film director, complete with his white panama hat and a shooting stick, had arrived.

Out to sea the fish were coming on board Johnny's ski boat as fast as they could bait the hooks.

In the kitchen of the restaurant, the hard slog was underway in preparation for the dinner that night which was being thrown in honour of *The Great Man*. Hector and Ricky were both rushing around amid the chopping and slicing.

Back at the campsite, Hank and Justine's parents were sensibly having a snooze; they were on holiday.

9

In the village, Fix received a second phone call from his friend in Umtata and listened carefully before making a decision.

"The description sounds correct," he spoke into the phone, "but I can't authorise a search warrant unless I am sure. Better send me a mug-shot on tomorrow's bus. The only thing he's done so far is take Johnny's charter but there is nothing illegal about honest competition. I can't quite imagine Aldo Carli turning out to be an Afrikaner from Benoni. I saw him only last night, and he looked very Italian to me the way he was chatting up the girls from the film set. Put the photograph on the morning bus."

TEN KILOMETRES out of Port St Johns the man in question was smiling to himself, his black van full to the brim with bulging black bags. In just sixteen hours, he was going to be rich and have enough money to buy his house in the south of Spain and live in the way he had always wanted to be accustomed. All girls liked rich men, and he chuckled happily to himself. He would catch the leopard for his friend the Sangoma and then get the hell out of the country, never having to work again. The life of a playboy appealed to him immensely.

WHEN JOHNNY KNEW they would not be able to sell any more fish, they pulled up the lines and headed for shore.

"That freighter still hasn't moved," he observed bringing the ski boat up onto the plane, both Yamahas on full throttle. Five minutes later, he headed straight for the beach and ran in fast through the small waves hitting the soft sand, the momentum pushing the ski boat right out of the water. Mac was waiting to help and a small crowd of holidaymakers soon gathered around the boat. Justine and Hank felt chuffed with themselves as they helped throw the good catch onto the sand.

When the fish were cleaned and washed in the sea and the boat pulled onto the trailer behind Johnny's Land Rover, Mac pulled from his jacket the list he had been given by Hector.

"Ten crayfish. Bucket of mussels. Two buckets of oysters... You two want to go diving?"

"Wait for me, Justine. I'll get your goggles," he told her. "Are we going to dive in the gully?"

"And below The Gap."

Hank just heard the words from behind as by then he was through the trees and heading for the camp. To go diving with Mac was the best thing in his life, just a fraction ahead of going fishing with Johnny.

A SHOAL of tiny fish swam below them as they snorkelled

through the gully, Mac leading with Justine and Hank on either side. On the right, the weed-encrusted rock dropped five metres to the floor of the gully waving its wands of bright green seagrass. Mac was watching for the smile of the oysters, the muscles in the oysters relaxing enough to suck in plankton: closed tight, the slipper oysters were almost invisible and looked like barnacled parts of the rock face. Mac pointed and dived, bringing up a big oyster. Hank dived and came up with nothing and all three of them surfaced and pushed their goggles onto their foreheads.

"Look for the smiles on the oysters and the feelers of the crayfish. Ready again?"

The shoal of tiny silver fish swam up to look at them and rushed past their masks, the breathing tubes gripped in their teeth. Mac tapped Justine on her arm and pointed at a big rock on the floor of the gully. He made the signal warning them to be ready to dive and pushed himself down into the water, holding his breath. The water buoyancy made the rock a fraction of its surface weight and when he pulled it away the crayfish hiding underneath scuttled in all directions pursued by Hank and Justine, Mac having taken two big ones the moment his hands were free of the rock.

"There were so many," spluttered Justine coming up for air. They were all laughing.

"Down again. We've an hour before the light goes. Six more big ones." The water was warm, and they reached their target of oysters and crayfish in half an hour.

"Now for the mussels. You tired?"

"Not a bit," beamed Hank who was near to exhaustion. "Show us where to go."

10

"Have you got them?" whispered Nteli. They were under the mango tree and it was pitch dark; the moon had yet to rise.

"Told dad we wanted to study the night sky," said Hank. They spoke in English for Justine's sake as she understood very little Xhosa.

"You'd better lead the way." Justine was also whispering. "It's so dark."

They walked over the bridge and worked their way round the back of the lagoon crouching carefully when they passed below the thatched house. The arc lights had not been turned on and Hank could see a lamp burning in the lounge. Someone walked out onto the stoep wearing boots; they froze, crouching low to the grass beside the path. The boots moved again, and they moved on, Nteli feeling his way along the path he knew so well. The path led them round the thatched house, and they climbed the wooden steps over the game fence into the nature reserve, Hank gripping his father's night binoculars firmly to prevent them from banging his chest.

"They haven't turned on the generator," whispered Hank.

"Must have finished those ski boats," said Justine. "What is he doing?"

"That's what we want to find out, Justine. The house just now was so quiet. They weren't even talking to each other."

"I think he spiked my drink."

"What?"

"He gave me a drink and it made me sick."

"That shows he's up to something," thought Hank, innocently.

The ground dropped away behind the house with tall grass on either side of the path but they still walked like conspirators, bent with caution. They walked down to the rocks and climbed back again to come at Nteli's rock-ship from the other side, away from the film people if any of them were still working on the set. Hank dislodged a small boulder by mistake and it crashed back behind them just missing Justine who was last.

"Sorry sis… Be careful," he warned Nteli in Xhosa who was in front. They were about to crest the high point and would be visible from the wreck of the *Bremen*.

"No one can see," assured Nteli. "Too dark." He could see the path now his eyes were fully adjusted and led them over the top onto the rock-ship with its shallow dip in the centre that gave protection from the wind and spray on bad nights. The rock was shaped like the prow of a liner and they had always imagined themselves out to sea when they sat in the lee of the sea-gouged walls. When the sea was really wild, it crashed over the walls and filled the middle like a swimming pool before the water gushed out the back. Hank adjusted the binoculars and trained them out to sea.

"Still there," he told them. "Hasn't moved. Doesn't make

sense. If the engine was badly damaged, they would have called for help. The sea can come up in hours and look what happened to the *Bremen* when it ran out of engine power." They could see the silent wreck down on the rocks to their left: the film crew had gone as quickly as they had come and the silhouette was once more of an old German warship. "That ship out there is up to something and my bet it's something to do with the Italian and those ski boats he's been fixing. Why does the ship anchor so far out? The answer lies inside the black bags you saw, sis, and we are going to find out. I think the man's a crook. You can always tell crooks."

"How?" said his sister, glad of the sweater now the breeze was coming off the sea.

"Don't you think he's a crook?"

"I think it's all in your imagination and I'm out here on a wild goose chase."

"You and Hector," and they all burst out laughing. Hank took a long look at the ship on the horizon that was showing the minimum of lights and passed around the glasses for the other two to have a look.

"It's sinister," shuddered Justine when it came to her turn.

"That's what I told you. You just feel they are crooks… Why does he go off all day in a closed panel van when he says he's a fisherman. We caught plenty. I'm going to have a look at that van."

"Nothing came out," said Nteli.

"What do you mean?"

"Some of us watched when he came back. Just put the van in the garage and shut the doors."

"Is the garage locked?"

"Never was."

"Come on. The generator's still silent."

The walk back was quicker as they did not crouch so low now they knew there was no one around but when they approached the garage down below the house, they found the door open and Nteli signalled them back.

"That door was shut when we came by just now," he whispered into Hank's ear.

"He's in there... I can hear something. Look, he's coming out, and he's carrying something heavy."

The silhouette of a man walked away down the road in the direction of the bridge.

"Let's follow him. It must be Aldo."

"What's he doing, do you think Hank?" asked Justine.

"As I said, that's what we're going to find out," and he led the pursuit, keeping a good distance behind the man who had now walked into the trees.

"He'll turn right and cross the bridge."

"Wrong," said Nteli whose eyes were better in the dark. "He's taken the path up into the forest!"

"Why didn't he wait for the moon to come up if he wanted to walk in the forest?" asked Justine who was always more practical. "Who wants to walk in the forest at night apart from Mad Martin?"

"Up to something," mumbled Hank. "Up to something."

"What can the forest have to do with the ship?" wondered Nteli. "You can't use a ski boat in the forest and that thing he's carrying is very heavy."

"It's a radio. Of course. He's going up to the top of the hill to signal."

"But Hank, he's got a ship-to-shore in his house. I saw the aerial and heard it," said Justine.

They followed in silence and the man ahead drew them further and further into the forest.

"This place is creepy at night," trembled Justine five minutes later. "Where's he going?"

"He's stopped. In the middle of the pathway. He's kneeling down."

"How can you see, Nteli?" asked Justine.

Hank brought up his father's naval glasses, and the picture sprang clearly into his vision. Aldo Carli was on his knees fixing a chain to the trunk of a stout tree.

"He's setting a trap," said Nteli.

Hank watched the man through his binoculars as he pulled back the jaws and set them in place. "What's he trapping, Nteli?"

"The leopard. Much muti in a leopard."

"He's coming back." Hank pulled up urgently, and they all shrank away from the path into the forest and let the Italian pass them in the dark on his way back before they all walked on to look at the trap.

In horror, Justine looked down on the jaws gaping ready to clutch a foot or a paw, "That could catch a man! What do we do?"

"Pee on the track and all around it. Animals don't like the smell of us humans."

Justine turned her back. "Men are so crude."

"But practical," Hank said doing what he had to do. When they reached the road, Hank turned right instead of following the road across the bridge.

"Now what?" snapped Justine.

"The van. We haven't looked in the van."

Together and very cautiously, they followed each other back along the dirt road.

"He's locked it. Now why's he locked it?" said Hank feeling the heavy padlock. "Nteli, you must set up a watch. Your gang must keep an eye on this house and come and wake us if anything happens. My bet is he's waiting for the moon to rise."

"Why?" asked his sceptical sister.

Hank shivered in the night.

"What's the matter, Hank?"

"Someone just ran over my grave."

"Don't be so macabre."

"What does that mean, Justine?"

"Look it up in the dictionary. Now, can I go home and have my supper? Aren't you tired?"

"Second wind."

"What's that?" asked Nteli and Hank did his best to translate into Xhosa as the three of them crossed the bridge and walked away from the danger zone.

$\mathcal{I}$t was cold that night on the rock-ship and Nteli lit a fire while they fished for the elusive crayfish. Two of his gang were in position near the thatched house, one of them ready to report back if anything stirred in the house. The moon was only due to rise in half an hour and the heavens were brilliant with three distinct layers of stars.

Hank climbed up onto the rock and put his wicker basket down next to the fire. He had eaten his supper and ostensibly gone off to catch crayfish with a bamboo pole.

"Anything happened, Nteli?"

"They're asleep. All the lights are out... We caught one crayfish, which we are going to roast on the fire. What's that?" they had spoken in Xhosa and he was pointing to the unusual-looking basket Hank had put down.

Pointing to a cross in the heavens, Hank said, "Nteli, just look at the sky. That must be the Southern Cross... Or is it that one?"

"What is it?" Nteli was inspecting the wickerwork.

"A basket. Sort of. It's going to make your life much easier and the gang will think you are a thorough wizard."

"There's rotten fish in the bottom... Where did you get it from?"

"My dad."

"There is no lid."

"Put your arm down that funnel and pull out the fish."
Nteli did as he was told and got his hand stuck inside the basket.

"I'm stuck."

"Exactly. Let go of the fish and use your free hand to push open the sticks, which make that funnel and you'll come free... That's it. Now, if a crayfish slides down that funnel to eat the fish he'll be unable to get out as crayfish do not have a spare hand or a brain. What we do is lower the crayfish pot down on this rope and pull it up when it's full. But you can only use it when the sea's calm like tonight."

"Why don't the crayfish eat the fish through the holes in the basket?"

"Their feelers are too short and the fish has been placed on wooden spikes in the centre of the basket."

"Who invented it? Your dad?"

"No. It was the fishermen in the Mediterranean thousands of years ago. They don't have bamboo poles in that part of the world."

"It won't work."

"We can only try."

The basket was lowered way down into the sea until it hit the sand bottom and then the end of the rope was tied to a rock.

MAD MARTIN WOKE when the moon shone directly onto his face and he lurched up out of his improvised bed and his one old blanket fell to the floor. The moonlight was penetrating directly through into his fallen down cottage and inspiration struck him with the force of lightning. Within seconds, he had the black cloak slung over his shoulders, the Underwood under his arm and he was off up the path into the forest heading for the source of his inspiration, the moon-bathed hippo fig tree deep in the forest.

The trap sprang exactly as meant to do and grabbed his leg at the knee sending the Underwood flying into the dark recesses of the trees with Mad Martin sprawling in agony on the path. After the first shock of pain, he desperately tried to pull open the jaws of steel but his brain would not function properly from the pain and twenty-five years of smoking dope, and he could not see what he was doing in the dark of the moon. In fear, pain and madness he howled like a dog and went on howling.

Mac came awake with the agonised sounds and ran barefoot into the forest thinking the leopard had taken a man but found Mad Martin struggling in the pathway instead. Using his great strength, he was able to prise open the jaws and release the leg.

"I will kill whoever laid a trap like that," he raged into the night sky. The inert Martin whose leg was mangled, the bone crushed, and the flesh ripped by the steel, lay whimpering.

The colony was awake as Mac walked through the trees to his cottage and put the man down on his own bed, pumped up the pressure lamp and looked at the leg more thoroughly.

"The bastards," he yelled. "The shock will kill him. Get some blankets," he commanded the crowd that had gathered, torches playing in the night.

"What did that?" demanded Johnny, pointing at Martin's leg.

"Jaw trap. Someone is after the leopards."

"It's Aldo Carli," began Hank who had run from the rock-ship with Nteli at the first howls. "We saw him set the trap and peed on it to stop the leopard. We didn't think anyone would walk in the forest at night."

"Is that helicopter still on the beach?" asked Mac.

"Yes," said someone from the back.

"Let's go," and Mac picked up the body well wrapped in blankets and strode towards the beach with torches playing the path to show him the way. "We've got to get him to Umtata Hospital."

THE MOMENT the helicopter took off from the beach, Mac, followed by a big crowd, made for the thatched house.

"*Aldo Carli*!" he bellowed. "*Aldo Carli*!" The house was in darkness.

"Anybody see him leave Second Beach?"

"The Land Cruiser is here."

"And the van's locked in the garage," said Hank.

"Let's go get him," Mac angrily said and marched onto the stoep intending to break down the French doors.

"You thinking of breaking and entering?" snarled a voice from the side of the house. "If you do, I will shoot you."

"Did you put down that trap?"

"I did. I also have a licence issued in Umtata. Reports show the leopard has killed two goats and four sheep."

"I'll break your neck."

"Please witness the threat," he entreated the crowd.

"Easy, Mac," calmed someone.

"You caught Mad Martin. He may die."

"That will do him a favour. Only a lunatic crashes through the forest at night. At first light, I would have neutralised the trap. He was lucky not to have been attacked by the leopard months ago. Now will you please leave my stoep or my men will throw you out."

12

*H*ank went to bed determined not to miss anything. He had given Nteli the torch and run a piece of string under the tent. Carefully, feeling his way in the dark he tied the other end to his right big toe.

"Go to sleep," growled his father.

"I am asleep," pretended Hank and pulled the blanket up to his chin and listened to the sounds of the bush outside the kombi tent. There was something very wrong at the thatched house. He called them his 'men' when threatening Mac and the way he had said it was not friendly to Mac or the men; and the men were meant to be his friends. One of the leopards coughed from up in the forest but Hank did not recognise the sound. There was a lot of fish-plopping noise coming from the river but the sea was silent. Hank fell asleep.

Four hours later Hank woke to a gentle tugging on his toe and felt down the camp bed to tug the string three times in response. He listened for a full minute but no one else in the tent was awake and very gently he pulled off the blanket and crawled out on his hands and knees. It was pitch black outside, and it took him a moment to pick out Nteli standing under the trees. The camp was fast asleep and even the dogs had stopped scavenging in the dustbins. An owl hooted in competition with a nightjar and crickets sang in the long grass. The stars were brilliant, and the moon was now down behind the hill as they walked in deep shadow following the path from instinct, as Hank could not even see his right hand when he held it out in front of him.

"They are loading the boats with black bags," whispered Nteli when they were out of the campsite. The night watchman was fast asleep in his box by the gate and his fire had long burnt down to ashes; there was a faint glow in the embers. "They started loading when the moon threw a shadow over the house."

Hank fingered the pocketknife in his trousers; he was going to cut a bag and find out what was inside. He shivered with mingled excitement and fear as they crossed the bridge, Nteli feeling for the edge of the concrete it was so dark. The stars twinkled brilliantly in the heavens but down on earth, the lights were out and everyone was fast asleep. The boys worked their way round to the garage where the double doors were wide open and one of Aldo's men was carrying two full black bags down to the beach where the three boats were prepared for launching. From the house, more black bags were being carried down to the boats and loaded into the holds, the men getting right inside to push the bags as far back as possible.

Hank waited till all three men from the house had gone back for more before moving quickly from under the trees, crossing the beach to the nearest boat, with Nteli following. He knew the white sand that had shown him the men, would also make him visible from the house, and he and Nteli dived into the boat crawling inside to the bow having picked the one that was being loaded last. On hands and knees in total darkness, Hank pulled the blade from his Swiss army knife his dad had given him for his fourteenth birthday and cut into a bulging bag that spilled leaves into the boat giving off a pungent smell.

"What is it?" whispered Hank.

"Dagga."

"So that's it. They are smuggling dagga out to that freighter. We must tell Mac. He'll know what to do. Come on," and he climbed backwards out of the hold and looked over the side of the boat to see one of the men crossing the last bit of sand on his way to their boat.

"Back," murmured Hank and scuttled back into the hold.

They heard the man board the boat, pushing his way inside to where they were hiding and shoved more black bags up against them. Another man climbed on and thrust his own bags inside the prow. Then, Aldo Carli gave the instruction to drop the wooden partition in place from the deck, compartmentalising the hold with its bags of dagga and the two boys.

"Thought we'd get more in the front hold," said one of the men as he locked the hatch.

"Hurry, we haven't got all night."

Hearing the men leave the boat, Hank felt the wood of the hatch just above his head.

"What do we do?" quaked Nteli, panic in his voice. He was a boy of the open spaces and did not even sleep in a hut.

"I don't know. There are holes drilled in the hatch. Must be for the fish. We won't suffocate."

"How do we get out?" he had tried pushing up the partition the man had locked into place. "Shall we shout?"

"Dagga smugglers are dangerous. We'll wait till daylight and then shout for help."

"I'm frightened, Hank."

"So am I."

THE LOADING WENT on for an hour without a break. Hank kept looking for light in the night sky through a five-centimetre hole immediately above his head but all he could see was the perfect definition of the Southern Cross, a patch of the Milky Way and a thousand stars. He mentally drew the line through the Cross to the pointer stars. "At least I know which are North and South," he whispered. It made him less disorientated. "What can they do to us, anyway?"

"Those people kill each other for money." Nteli had heard about drug smugglers.

In a short space of silence when Hank judged all three of the men had gone up to the house, he tried to pry at the catch that held the partition in place but the angle made it impossible to make any impression and he was frightened of breaking his blade: the knife was his only weapon. The smell of dagga from the split bag, made worse by the sweat from their bodies making it moist, was sickening.

The sound of the Land Cruiser starting was sudden and ominous in the night. The vehicle moved towards their boat where it was coupled to the trailer and they felt themselves being pulled round in a curve. From checking the Southern Cross Hank realised they had turned in a full circle and he knew they were being pushed out into the water.

"We are going out now," he breathed, his voice muffled by the diesel engine of the Land Cruiser. The wire that had pulled the boat onto the trailer was released and the boat slipped backwards into the sea. The boat came free of the trailer and the feeling of buoyancy ran through them.

"We're afloat," whispered Hank again.

Feet climbed into the boat and walked towards them: another man coughed right above their heads from where he was standing in the water holding the prow as he pushed it further into the sea. The other man pulled the rope connected to the starter motor and one of the engines fired and faded but he tried again bringing the engine to life. They headed out to sea in a due easterly direction on one engine, Hank again having checked the Southern Cross. The roll of the boat made it more difficult to cut the north to south line through the stars. They were sailing diagonally away from the north to south line straight to where the freighter had been anchored that afternoon when they were fishing. The second outboard engine was brought to life and their speed picked up.

"We seem to be towing something," said Hank from his experience with Johnny when they had towed a stricken tourist back to shore. "He's bringing those engines to full throttle but we haven't gone on the plane."

"Maybe he's towing the other two boats to cut down the noise, or they didn't fix the engines in time."

"You should go back to school, Nteli."

"Why?"

"You are wasted as a fisherman. You are exactly right. They've filled the other two boats from the van and the house and are using them like dead barges. That freighter doesn't want to stay out there forever or they'll be reported. There's a lot of sea traffic up the Wild Coast. It's the main shipping lane up the African coast after the ships round the Cape."

"How will they know we are out on the sea? No one saw us. Did anyone hear you leave the tent?"

"They were all sound asleep. Your gang?"

"They know I went to wake you but none of them think very much for themselves. Why I run the gang. I'm hungry. I didn't even get any of the crayfish."

By the time the engines were cut back and their speed dropped even slower, Hank thought the night sky was paling fractionally and then they bumped the side of an iron vessel and a line of rope crashed down just above their heads and made them duck.

"Push the bags away from the prow and with any luck they won't find us when they unload."

Men were coming on board speaking a language neither Hank nor Nteli understood and the business of transferring the black bags began. Ten minutes later when Hank was sure the dawn was breaking in the sky, the catch that held their board in place was released. The flow of sweet sea air flowed into the small hold and they heard the black bags being removed from in front of them. Instinctively they pulled back against the bulkhead trying to roll themselves into as small a ball as possible that would not be seen in the fork of the prow. There were four bags left when the argument started, men cursing each other, the tone of voice understandable if not the language: they had found the split bag.

"What's that?" they heard Aldo say in Afrikaans all trace of his Italian accent left on shore.

"One of the bags has split, Kobus."

"Give it to me... This bag is not split. Someone's cut it with a knife." The boys could see a torch playing into the boat and they could see a pair of legs, and then a man crouched down to look into the hold and shone the torch right into Hank's face blinding him.

Using the back of the boat like a starting block, Hank shot forward past the last bags of dagga, the Swiss army knife held rigidly at arm's length. He plunged the knife behind the light of the torch and felt the blade sink into flesh: the torch crashed to the deck and went out but Hank was still blinded by the intense light that had shone into his eyes.

"I've been stabbed," shrieked Kobus Kriel, alias Aldo Carli, and tried to grab Hank who was trying to see where to put in a second stab.

Nteli had not looked directly into the torch and following Hank out of the hold, kicked at the man with the intention of scoring a goal from fifty metres. Kobus lost his balance with the impact and fell into the water, the rip in his thigh from the knife-wound colouring the sea. They could see him in the water as they both looked over the side, the grey dawn gave sufficient light for them to see, the black spots in Hank's eyes having faded. There was a thud from the back of the boat as one of the men jumped from the *barge* ski boat and a seaman dropped from the freighter, almost landing on top of Nteli. With two hefty blows, the seaman knocked Nteli and Hank to the deck, the Swiss army knife slithering away.

"Get him out," shouted the man from the *barge*. "There are sharks in this water and he's bleeding."

Kobus, his lifejacket keeping him afloat, swam to the side and pulled himself back on board: he was very strong and the cut in his thigh was doing a lot of bleeding but very little else.

"What's happening?" called down the Greek captain in English and one of the *barge* men replied in Greek. A steel rope ladder was thrown down the rusted side of the freighter and Hank was picked up under the man's arm like a sack of mealies, the man expertly judging the rocking boat before grabbing the ladder. Kobus picked up the still inert Nteli and followed, but not before pocketing Hank's knife lying in the corner of the deck.

"Hand up the last of the bags," he said looking back from halfway up the rope ladder. The third man had climbed into the lead ski boat and had loaded the black bags into a rope-net that was being used to pull the dagga up to the freighter where it was quickly disappearing below deck into a false bulkhead next to the engine room, above the diesel tanks. By the time the two boys were thrown onto the hard deck of the freighter there was no sign of the contraband cargo and the captain was giving instructions to have the ship put underway.

The Greek captain would have killed a grown man who gave him a problem but back on the island of Rhodes in the Greek archipelago, he had seven sons of his own, the reason for his shipping dope in the first place as education was expensive in any part of the world. The boys gained consciousness and looked up at the captain who was clearly visible now the sun had rimmed up out of the ocean and was showering the surrounding sea with light and colour. The three empty ski boats had been allowed to drift, their value paid for a thousand times over; they would drift for days in the Mozambique current and eventually smash up on the coast, and Aldo Carli would be reported as lost at sea and the police would look in vain for his body. The boys were shivering with fright and cold.

"Shut them in my day cabin," ordered the captain to his first lieutenant and then turned to Kobus. "Better put something on that cut." He was smiling. "That's a nasty cut.

Not so clever a big man like you being cut up by a little boy like that."

"He is not so little."

"Maybe not. Now let us get away from this part of the coast. We've stayed two days too long already."

13

The freighter sailed away from the African coast and out of the shipping lanes before turning south. The boys searched the captain's day cabin, found nothing out of the ordinary and lost interest. They were hungry and thirsty, the taste of the split bag of dagga still lingering at the back of their throats.

"You think that basket of yours has caught any crayfish?" asked Nteli. Hank made no reply. "Where are we going?"

"To the other side of the world. Probably to Europe. My grandad came from Europe on my mother's side. Dad's family haven't been to Europe for hundreds of years. You want to see Europe, Nteli?"

"Not like this. They'll throw us into the sea when they are far enough away."

"You think they'd do that? Look at this," and he pointed at the window which showed them a round view of the deck outside. "I can open this window and climb on deck."

"What can you do on deck?"

"Nothing. There's someone coming."

"I told you they were going to throw us into the sea."

The door opened, and a steward brought a tray of food and put it down on the captain's table. "Captain's compliments," he said in heavily accented English and left the room, turning the lock when he shut the door.

"I don't think they'll throw us overboard, Nteli. Why feed us if they are going to feed us to the fish?"

Nteli was not listening having pushed a large piece of bread and cheese into his mouth. They ate until nothing was left and then drank their milk. Sitting back in the captain's best chair Hank felt comfortably full, his eyes lazily looking around the walls of the cabin and coming back to a large wooden box attached to the wall beside the door. He got up, lifted the latch and pulled open the lid to the box.

"What are those?" Nteli was leaning over his shoulder looking into the box.

"Distress flares... If we see another boat through the porthole, I'm going to fire one of these." Systematically he opened every draw and every cupboard, even pulling up the carpet to have a look underneath which was when they discovered something interesting. Under the captain's desk was a square cut into the deck with indents at either side large enough for fingers to pry up the small handles. Quickly, they prised up the handles and the two boys got a grip, one on each side of the square and pulled. Inside was the radio the captain used to send his own private messages when he did not wish for the ship's radio operator to know what he was sending.

"It's a radio for sending signals in Morse code. Must be very old. You tap out a message on that knob. Works off that battery."

"What are you doing?" asked Nteli. Hank was tapping the same sequence on the knob, pausing, and sending again.

"I only know the sequence of SOS. Why didn't I listen

when the scoutmaster was telling us how to make words… I'll send an SOS every half an hour."

FIFTY-FIVE MINUTES later they heard a helicopter and Hank craned his neck up to have a look.

"It's trying to land on the ship. There's a sort of ladder out of the cockpit door and someone's holding on to the end about two metres below the chopper." Hank waited for the chopper to come back into his line of vision. "The man's now six metres below the chopper but the ship's crew are moving to the other side of the boat."

Hank ran back to the box, pulled out three distress flares and with difficulty opened the porthole window, and put his head out of the cabin.

"Give me a shove. If my head goes through so should the rest. Then I'll pull you out."

With Nteli pushing from behind, Hank wriggled his body at right angles to the floor and began to worm his way forward and out of the porthole. No one was in sight as the living quarters gave out onto a small corridor and with the crew on the other side of the ship, he dropped unseen headfirst towards the deck finally pulling his arms free from behind as Nteli lowered him to the deck by his feet. There was a lot of shouting from the other side and he picked up the flares he had dropped on deck before putting his head through the porthole and put them in his windcheater jacket. He then helped Nteli out of the captain's day cabin.

"The ship's being boarded," and he fired a flare out to sea.

"Shoot them!" he heard Kobus shout as the boys came out on deck and climbed up the ladder to get on top of the day cabin where they would be able to signal the helicopter without being seen by the men below. The man on the trapeze saw them and signalled his pilot before letting himself fall forward, his legs curled snugly at the knees over the pole letting his hands hang free.

"Put up your arms with your palms open and when I grab you below the elbow, grab my arms at the same time."

"He really was a catcher in the circus," said Hank looking up at Hector hanging upside down from the improvised trapeze. "You go first Nteli. Quick. Hold up your arms. He's going to snatch you. I've seen them do it in the circus."

The helicopter came back and Nteli was snatched from the roof of the cabin and swung away from the ship. A shout went up from the deck and Hank went to the side while the improvised trapeze, with Hector holding on by his knees and Nteli gripped arm locked to arm, was winched up to the chopper that hovered thirty metres from the ship. A rope was slid down over Hector's back and the loop hitched under Nteli's feet and tightened when it reached his armpits where it took his weight and he was pulled up into the helicopter. Hector swung himself back up to sit on the trapeze and rest his arms.

Hank could now see Johnny's boat alongside the freighter with his father and Mac trying to get aboard. Kobus saw Hank up on the cabin roof and broke away to climb the steel ladder that would bring him up to Hank who was looking back at the chopper as Hector readied himself for the second run. Running back to the rail, Hank pulled a distress flare from his pocket and fired it down at Kobus who was halfway up the ladder. A burning line of phosphorus caught the smuggler's hair sending Kobus crashing down to the deck where he rolled over, still on fire, and jumped over the ship's rail into the sea. Hank watched

Hector carefully; keeping his arms stretched above his head, he felt the shock as his arms were almost pulled from their sockets as he was snatched from the roof.

"Just hold on lad," said Hector's voice half a metre above his head. "And don't look down." The hands that gripped Hank's arms were made of steel and he managed to smile at the upside-down face above him. Feeling the noose of the rope searching for his legs, he kept them tightly together without having to be told, with his toes pointing down. Then the noose was coming up around his body and the rope took hold under his arms.

"Let go your right hand," instructed Hector. "It's holding!" he shouted and let go the other hand and watched Hank being winched up into the helicopter as he pulled himself up into a sitting position.

"*Scram!*" he shouted down to Johnny. "*We've got both of them!*"

"You want to come up?" asked Strider who was working the winch.

"Not yet. I like the sensation of the trapeze again."

"Hector, you must have been good?"

"Didn't get anyone killed."

Down below, Johnny had his ski boat on full throttle and circled away from the freighter as the Greek crew pulled a burnt Kobus out of the water.

"What a pity," said Hector to himself. "You never find a shark when you want one."

Nteli's big black eyes shone brighter than the morning sun: he had never ridden in a helicopter before and the experience was both awe-inspiring and frightening at the same time. Down below at thirty knots, Johnny was cutting a vast V in the ocean in a direct line back to Second Beach some fourteen kilometres away. From aloft, the pilot could see the horizon but Johnny was blind, pushing the sea boat along the line set by the helicopter. Strider was checking his sixteen-millimetre movie camera and smiling happily to himself: Strider spent most of his day smiling as he enjoyed his job and his life.

Back in the helicopter, Hector was massaging his arms that had not been used so strenuously since he left the European leg of the circus tour. He was glad he would not have to do another performance; his arms were not what they used to be. He looked round and gave the boys a wry smile: the engine noise was too loud for any form of conversation. Behind and below them the freighter kept on its course taking it as far from African waters as possible at its maximum speed of seventeen knots, which meant it was doing very little in the line of a quick escape.

Second Beach drew closer and closer and the little dots became people and they could see *The Great Man* sitting in his chair and the action on the *Bremen* and the other crowd waiting for them at the water's edge, and back between the trees, Hank made out a police truck.

14

The boys' legs were rubbery when they jumped down onto the soft sand and Justine ran to hug her brother.

"What's that for?" asked Hank as if nothing had happened.

Nteli's gang were also on the beach, off a bit from the main crowd but they were not kicking a football. A lot of white teeth were visible when they saw Nteli climb out of the helicopter. One of the gang tapped the football in his direction and he kicked it as hard as possible sending it soaring halfway down the beach. The ski boat came ashore with the Yamahas screaming, their propellers out of the water until Johnny went back to the outboards and cut the engines. Hank and his father shook hands like old friends and his mother was crying silently.

"What happened, dad?"

"Did you find out what was in the bags?" interrupted Fix.

"Dagga. They were smuggling dagga."

"You will swear to that?"

"So will Nteli. We were trying to find out what was in the bags when they closed the hold."

Fix was walking away swiftly towards the police truck where the Chief of Police and the Army Commander were waiting next to the radio.

"Fix had a mugshot sent down from Umtata," said Hank's father. "Aldo Carli turned out to be Kobus Kriel, wanted by the South African and Transkei police. He had been on Police File three times but no one on Second Beach has a TV and the reception in Port St Johns is terrible. The police arrived with a warrant for his arrest soon after the sun came up and while they were searching the thatched house, they heard your SOS. One of Nteli's gang had seen him climb into the ski boat and not come out again and told the police where you had gone. With your SOS we pieced together that it came from the freighter."

Hank broke away from his father giving him a quick smile and ran down to the water.

"Don't take the boat out," he called to Johnny and Mac.

"You got some more bright ideas," teased Johnny. "You want to go fishing? I don't believe this young man," he said to Mac who was more conscious of Justine in her teeny-weeny white bikini than he should have been.

"Johnny, if a boat is adrift in the high sea, and there is no one aboard, can't you claim it?" he was gabbling so fast, Mac asked him to try the sentence all over again.

"Yes. Sort of," said Johnny the second time around. "There's the law of salvage. If I save a ship from the sea, I can claim a percentage of its value."

"There are three ski boats drifting ten kilometres from here. Once they had the dagga on board, they cut the boats adrift."

"Let's go," began Johnny getting the drift indeed.

"There's a big can of petrol in the Land Rover," he told Mac. "Three ski boats! Hey, Mac, we're going to be rich."

"Nteli!" shouted Hank.

"They'll be drifting down the Mozambique current," Johnny was saying to himself.

Ten minutes later Johnny's ski boat was back on the plane, heading out to sea, life jacket securely tied to the back and front of the four passengers. Johnny made for where he had seen the freighter anchored the previous day and cut the engines.

"Once I know the direction of the current, we'll turn on the motors. No boats around here," he went on, glassing the sea with a pair of binoculars. "Current is drifting at four knots up towards the Natal coast. Why the freighter didn't get far this morning sailing into the current after getting over the horizon. Give the motor a pull, Mac."

They rode to the roar of the outboards for ten minutes and Johnny cut back the power and came off the plane to search the sea again.

"Have a look," he said handing the glasses to Mac while pointing ahead.

"There's something in the sea," Mac looked for a moment and handed the binoculars to Hank. "Too far away. Looks like buoys but there's a long row of them. The current's bringing them our way."

Johnny opened the throttle and headed the ski boat at full power, the wake creaming behind the Yamahas, the propellers deep in the water. Fifty metres away Johnny dropped power, and the hull settled in the water sending a wake towards the line of objects floating in the sea; the buoys began to bob as the waves reached them.

"It's the dagga," cried Hank. "Those are black bags. They've thrown the dagga into the sea."

"Maybe the captain threw the fake Italian into the sea with his goons," Mac wistfully hoped.

"He's thrown out the evidence," said Hank.

"Someone's going to have fun when that lot washes ashore," grinned Johnny.

"Hank, how soon before we found you did they cast the boats adrift?"

"An hour, maybe less."

"And it's forty minutes since we broke contact with the freighter. We should have sighted the ski boats unless they were cast adrift out of the Mozambique current. The captain must have been further out and once everything seemed normal, he was sailing back into the shipping lane when we found him. Those ski boats are further out to sea, out of South African waters."

"Does it make any difference to the salvage?" asked Hank.

"Just means we've further to tow them back but the lead boat had engines and petrol. Enough to get back to shore if they'd missed the freighter."

Nteli saw the boats first having the best eyesight on board and Johnny came off the plane to look through the glasses.

"Let's get a tow on them," said Johnny, lowering the glasses. "What a pleasure."

WHEN THE LINE of boats came into shore, the beach was crowded with the film crew and holidaymakers. An hour later, Johnny was laying his legal claim to the salvage in Fix's office.

"You think he'll claim his property?" queried Johnny.

"Not this one," said Fix looking at the mugshot of Kobus

Kriel. "Our friend won't be coming back to Port St Johns. Interpol have been notified and *SAS Emily Hobhouse* is looking for the freighter."

LATER THAT DAY, back at the rock-ship, Nteli was pulling up the contraption they had lowered into the sea the previous night.

"Does it feel heavy?" asked Hank.

"Maybe."

"Here it comes. Look at that, Nteli, it's full of crayfish and something else. Pull it up, man. Hurry!"

The wicker trap came up dripping seawater and was finally pulled onto the rock by willing hands. Inside, along with six fine crayfish was another fish with big, goo-goo eyes.

"It's an octopus," laughed Hank. Out of the wicker, tentacles were feeling around in the unaccustomed sunlight. Nteli, Hank and the gang broke up laughing.

"Beats a pole and string any day," decided Nteli.

15

he Great Man's Bedouin tent was a magnificent affair strewn with Persian and Afghan rugs with oriental copperware placed strategically on the carpets; incense was burning in two vessels hung from the roof of the tent and everything shouted taste and wealth. Even on location, *The Great Man* projected his image and the tent and its furnishings were well portrayed in the women's magazines of the world.

Strider put the movie into the projector, let down the screen at the opposite end of the tent and let the film role. Neither of them spoke as they watched the clips of Hector snatching first Nteli and then Hank from the tiny roof of the captain's day cabin. There was a good shot of Aldo Carli's hair sizzling after the flare had shot past the top of his head on his way up the ladder to get at Hank. There was a picture of Mac warding off boarders from Johnny's ski boat. And then, there was the film of the triumphant landing on Second Beach and *The Great Man* shouted, "*Stop*! Who's that woman?"

"Ah?" sighed Strider. "You see as well."

"What I see is the perfect woman. Run it again." The film slid back and resumed.

"Sensational. Who is she?"

"The boy's sister. Her name is Justine van Heerden. She is just about the most beautiful sixteen-year-old in the world."

"Play it again." The film was restarted. "Nonsense," snorted *The Great Man*. "That's a woman not a girl. Sixteen, my foot!"

"Seventeen in three weeks."

"Go and see her parents. She does have parents?"

"Yes. The woman hugging the boy is the mother."

"Good looking mother."

"The older man holding the boat in the surf is the relieved father... I hate drug smugglers. Can we use the clip?"

"Sadly, not in this movie. I want a screen test done on that girl... The perfect beauty in a woman lasts for so short a time," he smiled faintly. "It is the one thing we can capture on film forever. So photographic. I will write a script with this coast as the setting. The purity of women. So fresh. I will make her a worldwide sensation. My word, did lending them that helicopter pay off in the end? That restaurant man must have been one hell of a trapeze artist. Not many stunt men I know could do that first time round. Take his name."

"I asked him. He wants to stay retired."

"The things you find in out of the way places."

"I AM TOTALLY against children growing up too quickly," said Mrs van Heerden for the third time, causing Strider to change his approach.

"It's not only the film industry which has the problem. A lot of tennis players find themselves at a peak early in life. We could hold for a year but the director wants something on film to show his partners in America. I never saw him so excited."

They were seated in the kombi over a cup of tea, Mr van Heerden having gone off to fish. Justine, coming back from the beach for lunch heard Strider's voice and wondered what he was doing in the kombi with her mother. She coughed politely.

"Not interrupting anything am I, Mother?" Justine innocently put her head into the vehicle where her resolute mother was squaring off against the American cameraman. "Hi Strider!"

"Hi Justine. I was talking to your mother about you. *The Great Man* wants you to take a film test."

"Wow! Whatever for? Why me?"

"No sixteen-year-old daughter of mine is going off filming in America," pronounced Mrs van Heerden flatly.

"I'm seventeen next month. What's it all about?"

Strider explained his filming of the beach scene but Justine's mother became more adamant than ever.

"Opportunities like this rarely come twice in life," Strider patiently explained getting up. "Thanks for the tea. I hope the little lady doesn't regret it in a few years' time. What are you going to do when you leave school?"

"Secretarial college," interjected Mrs van Heerden. "Girls these days have to earn a living."

"She'll do that in the movie business. My word she will. Brooke Shields made millions before she turned sixteen and then went on to college. There was a picture in *Time* magazine the other day showing her in cap and gown. We would look after Justine, sure about that. Now, if you'll excuse me I've got some camerawork to do on board that old wreck. Glad your son got away, Mrs van Heerden."

"Thank you again."

"Thank the director. He lent the chopper. That man Hector's a real highflyer... You know it's got to be the most beautiful day I ever knew," he said out of the kombi. "Beats California every time."

16

*N*teli was terrified: Chief Munongo wanted to see him and there was no getting out of that one; the Transkei system of government was partially feudal and the word of the Chief had been law for as many generations as anyone could remember in Port St Johns. He climbed into the battered half-ton truck and sat down next to a large pig that was far too fat to try to jump out of the bakkie. They looked at each other with mild curiosity as the clutch was let out badly, lurching pig and boy in a heap to the back, the pig squealing in a high-pitched alarm. Nteli crawled onto his knees and managed a forlorn wave at the mango tree and his disconsolate gang who was staring down the road at him disappearing with the pig. By the time Nteli had helped the pig back onto its trotters, the truck had climbed away from the area of white settlement and they were headed up through the escarpment that led away from the river mouth and First Beach.

The Chief, when Nteli was confronted by him, was as fat as the pig, as if there was no more fat that could go under the skin. Nteli was suitably impressed as he had never met his Chief before, and the size of the man was in direct proportion to his wealth. In rural Africa, skinny people were poor, skinny like Nteli whose rib cage was showing quite clearly under the recently washed (thankfully) shirt that made up his wardrobe. As he approached the huge man seated on a three-legged stool outside of his hut, none of Nteli's thoughts were good, as anyone who had interfered in his life before had been bad news for him. To his surprise and considerable consternation, the Chief gave him a sunny smile and a ho-ho chuckle that sent the mounds of fat surrounding the man into convulsions. The driver of the truck, who still had him by the ear, let go, and with only his eyes Nteli looked right and left for a way to escape and get back to the sanctuary of his mango tree.

"Why are you not at school?" asked the Chief which confirmed Nteli's worst fears.

"I do not have the twenty-four rand a year... And who would feed me?" he added as an afterthought.

"But you are rich. They tell me you're a rich boy. You own boats. They even tell me if they catch the smuggler, which they will, there is a big reward. A very big reward. You were brave like your forefathers. That is good. Good boys must go to school."

"What about my gang?"

"They will go with you. You will pay. School will be easy for a boy who speaks English."

"How did you know?"

"They tell me... They tell me everything. Bright boys grow into clever men. Clever men help the Transkei. I will be your new father to see you work properly. The new term starts in Umtata in twelve days' time. This man will take you with your friends."

"Where will we live?"

"It is arranged."

As he was being driven back in the truck minus the pig, the deep-sea fishing rod in his mind began to disappear and he wondered if his friends would ever play football with him again.

17

---

*G*ushing water from her superstructure as she broke from the sea, *SAS Emily Hobhouse* surfaced next to the Greek freighter. Within minutes, the conning tower was open, and twenty sailors lined the top of the boat confronting the freighter, R1 automatic rifles ready for immediate use.

"We wish to come aboard," shouted the First Lieutenant which brought the Greek captain to his own rail. "We're coming aboard," which caused the Greek to shrug his shoulders and flick his fingers in an order, making the lieutenant glance quickly over the freighter. Instead of a confrontation, the same steel rope ladder that had carried Hank and Nteli up to the ship, was thrown over the side and clanged harshly against the rust of the hull. The sailors were then ordered to sling their rifles and board the ship behind the First Lieutenant.

"You have this man aboard?" he said showing the Greek captain a picture of Kobus Kriel, alias Aldo Carli that had been transmitted to *SAS Emily Hobhouse* electronically.

"Who is he?" asked the Greek innocently.

"Drug smuggler they say. My business is to hand him over to the police."

"Not on this ship."

"We'll have to search."

"Search as you like."

"I have a warrant to search for dagga. You're in South African waters."

"I know where I am."

"I want the dope and I want the man," shouted the officer to his men.

"You've all got a photograph so use it." The Greek had strolled to the rail and was looking down on the sleek power of the South African submarine.

"Wouldn't go down in one of them coffins, not on your life," he said to no one in particular. He had scrubbed clean first lieutenants for breakfast more than once in his career. The crime in life, he told himself is getting caught, and he had no intention of getting caught, today or any other day.

An hour later, the sailors regrouped on the deck of the freighter with not a leaf of dagga or sight of the man.

"Assemble your crew, captain," the First Lieutenant addressed the Greek. The motley looking lot came up from below including the two Greeks who had repaired the ski boats on Second Beach but who now blended perfectly with their fellow mates, two days of black growth on their unshaven faces. The lieutenant paced the inspection himself and ordered a final search of the ship to no avail. Kobus Kriel was not aboard.

18

The leopards had left the sanctuary of the hippo fig tree, the male leading his new wife on a hunt for something better than rock rabbits, it not being the male's habit of being satisfied with small things. He took his lady up into the hills well behind the Second Beach colony having judged correctly from a long distance that the craggy rocks would be home to more than one troop of baboon. It was a beautiful day.

STRIDER HAD BECOME as much infatuated with Justine as she was with Mac.

"Mac," said Strider, sitting over a beer in Mac's cottage, the day's shoot in the can, the weather still gentle, a cloudless blue sky free of wind, the sea just lapping at the hull of the *Bremen*. "You think you could read the man's lines for Justine. An offer like this from *The Great Man* is rare, you must see that."

"She's not quite seventeen," chuckled Mac. "Still a child. Lots of time."

"She doesn't look like a child to me."

"I know Justine. She still wants to go off diving with her brother. That kind of thing."

"But if I have a screen test on file, we can come back when she's older. She's about to finish her matric year, a year ahead of her age."

"Is she? Bright girl. What's in that script?" and he put out his hand and took the five pages reading them quickly. "This is a love scene, Strider," his eyes widening as he looked up at him.

"You know her from a small girl, Mac. Parents never see when their kids have grown up. She may not look a woman to you but she does to everyone else."

"And you want me to say these things to her in front of a camera?"

"Yes. They're good. *The Great Man* writes good dialogue."

"You've gotta be joking."

"Never more serious. You think about it. If you do the test with Justine, her parents will agree. You think about what this could do to the girl's life. Don't think about those lines as anything but fiction. You two would look good together on screen. You want another of these beers?"

"Sounds like bribery."

"You can sure bet your last dollar that's just what it is."

"You nearly finished the shoot?"

"One more morning."

"You'll get it." Mac was looking out to sea.

"Then we shoot the test on the veranda of the thatched house. Perfect setting. Palm trees, soft sand. Lots of sea. Blue skies. What else do lovers want?" and Strider broke into raucous laughter at Mac's expression of shock. "In the script. It's only a script.... I like this place of yours," he said sitting back looking at the bougainvillea, the stinkwood tree high above them, the two bantams ready to roost and the cat watching Mac, it's paws tucked up under its fur. Mac leant forward and stroked the animal and the cat began to purr.

"So do I," agreed Mac. "This place is paradise."

"Do you know how lucky you are?"

"I thank my maker every day..." He looked around at everything as he did so often. "Thanks for the beer. Cheers."

"Cheers, Mac. You're going to do that test for me?"

"What can I say with your beer to my lips?"

"Yes," said Strider smiling a little crookedly.

"Why not? I'll have a word with her parents."

CURIOUSLY, Nteli's pronouncement that the gang was going to school in ten days' time was received with smiles when he explained where the money was coming from. It appeared they had all had enough of playing football and that going to school was a bigger adventure than catching crayfish on the end of a long piece of string. The word *school* had sprung for them a future full of good things and the chance of one day living like Hank and Justine. The dream was there and the magic of school could bring it to them.

"And we can still come here during the holidays," said Nteli, happily surprised with their reaction.

"And we'd be together," said the youngest who was only nine. "You will still look after us, won't you Nteli?" his big black eyes were suddenly brimming with tears at the thought of being left on his own.

Nteli ruffled his head but said nothing, the big lump in his throat stopping any kind of sound. He looked up at the mango tree and wondered what life would bring them.

19

The Greek captain had not been as squeamish with Kobus Kriel as he had been with Nteli and Hank. The freighter had headed for South African waters after throwing the black bags into the sea, first waiting for darkness, and had briefly anchored off the coast while Kobus was told to climb down the rope ladder over the side of the hull and get lost, his appeal against predator sharks falling on deaf ears. Finally, the rope ladder had been shaken by two strong seamen and Kobus had fallen into the night sea, and the freighter had got under way and headed out for its subsequent boarding by the *SAS Emily Hobhouse*.

Kobus had spent two hours in the water, every second expecting a shark to take off his legs. The luck of the devil saw the current sweep him in a wide arc and finally push him through the surf and wash him up on a lonely, Wild Coast beach thirty kilometres south of Second Beach. When he coughed the last of the water from his lungs, crawling on hands and knees up the beach, he swore to get his revenge. Everything had gone; his wealth, his dreams and probably his freedom and the only thing left was revenge on the kids who had taken his money and washed him up on a beach kilometres from anywhere, cold, coughing and penniless. The luck of the devil again provided a warm night, and he huddled in a small cave under the cliff shivering with shock and cursing in Afrikaans, swearing his revenge and imagining it's sweetness. He was going to kill them both. Nothing else would assuage his hatred.

When the sun came up in the morning and flooded his cave, he took coherent stock of his position. In his trouser pocket was a wet packet of Camel cigarettes that he threw away in disgust, a box of matches that he put in the sun to dry and the Swiss army knife that Hank had dropped and last seen slipping away across the deck of the *barge*. The castaway looked at the knife, pulled out the longest blade and felt the warm flush of revenge surge through his body: it cleared his brain. He would walk up the coast; he remembered the story of Mac walking from Cape Town. He could live from the sea and there was water in the rivers that fed the Wild Coast. Carefully picking up his by now dry matches, he began the walk. He was barefoot, his trouser leg gashed where Hank had stuck his knife, his shirt open as the buttons had torn away when they had shaken him free from the rope ladder head first down into the sea. After the boys, he would think about the Greek captain.

AFTER TWO MORE BEERS, Mac was sufficiently mellow to be led off by Strider to the van Heerden's campsite where the opposition to the film test collapsed in minutes. Strider gave the participants a script each and told them to read it through carefully and then come up to the thatched house where he would have the equipment ready for them. He left before anyone could change their minds or have cold feet, and half an hour later, with the light still perfect, Mac (hamming it up having taken a little wine from the van Heerdens) and Justine acted out the script on the stoep of the thatched house, the soundtrack picking up the hadedas on their way home to roost.

HAVING SET off to walk the thirty kilometres one hour after sunrise, Kobus Kriel was in time to watch the last of the sequence and he knew by the ease with which they were occupying his house that he was a fugitive. He shrank back into the coastal forest behind his old house to make a plan to fulfil the need for revenge. Skirting the back of the house, he found the track that took him to the path and the hippo fig tree that nobody visited with Mad Martin still recovering in the Umtata Hospital. Wearily, as it had been a tough walk in bare feet over the sand and along the paths that skirted the cliffs, he sat down with his back to the tree. An hour later, at dusk, the male leopard found him, causing Kobus to climb a stinkwood tree at considerable speed. The leopards (the female caught up with him when she heard the commotion) were both well fed on baboon and climbed up on top of the hippo fig tree and went to sleep side-by-side, very content with their lives.

WHEN *THE GREAT MAN* saw the rush, he was impressed.

"The way she says she loves the big man, you'd think she did. Born actress. Quite magnificent. Put her under a three-year contract. The man's not bad either."

"He was slightly drunk."

"That explains the acting," and they both laughed happy with the situation for different reasons. Strider had quickly calculated that Justine would be twenty-one at the end of the contract.

"She really gets it across when she says she loves him," he agreed, blind to the reality.

WHEN IT WAS COMPLETELY DARK, Kobus climb down the stinkwood making his way back to the thatched house, finding it empty but the back door to the kitchen wide open. For five minutes, he crammed food into his mouth and then went to look for a clean pair of socks and a pair of shoes. He thought of a hot bath but his need for revenge was stronger. He left the house the back way unseen by anyone. First, he was going to settle with the little black boy and then he would go after the white. He would wreak havoc and bring down the whole colony on top of him but he cared nothing for the consequence.

NTELI AND HANK had made a small fire in the centre of their rock-ship as much to keep them warm later on as to roast a bag of mussels they had picked off the rocks before the light faded. Low tide was at seven o'clock and they had climbed on the rock at half-past six to drop their crayfish baskets in exactly the right spots, the new moon showing them just enough to see what they were doing. Meanwhile the gang were fishing for crayfish with bamboo poles. The second wicker basket had taken three days to make, from collecting the reeds to weaving the basket. There were no lights on the ocean and without the weak moon and the twinkling night stars, everything on earth was as black as pitch except for their guttering fire that was having a time of it with a stiff, on-shore breeze.

"Weather will change tomorrow afternoon," said Nteli, feeling the new direction of the wind on his left cheek.

THE FIRST PLACES Kobus Kriel checked were the campsite and the mango tree. He found the kombi and even had a look in through the driver's side window but there was nobody about. He circled back along the river, as if he was out for an evening stroll should anyone ask what he was doing in the dark, finding the mango tree still alone. Making his way over the bridge and through the trees he moved very quietly past Mac's cottage from where there was neither light nor sound; he could just make out the stable door, the bottom half bolted and the top left open, which was Mac's habit when he was away from home. People were disinclined to steal from a man who stood six feet six inches in his bare feet.

Kobus Kriel moved past the cottage on the other side of the path keeping to the rough lawn that stopped his feet from making any kind of sound. Finding the right path, he circled up behind his own house on his way to the big rock where he knew the black kids caught their crayfish.

MAC HAD BEEN LYING in his hammock, his pipe dead as he had run out of tobacco and money. Every muscle in his body ached from sawing up trees to make into seats for Hector to put under the milkwood trees beside the beach. The sixty rand he had been promised would come in handy. Watching the shadow pass the bougainvillaea bush, he assumed it was a black man on his way home to Third Beach as the path was a shortcut to the game fence that started the nature reserve. Another shadow passed causing Mac to strain his night eyes to the full but the thin slither of moon was on the other side of the tall bougainvillaea and what the shadow seemed to be was a man on all fours moving along the path. This puzzled Mac as the man was making not a sound, moving not one stone on the gravel path, and then the *man* cut the onshore wind whilst Mac lay motionless in his hammock.

"Leopard," Mac told himself, freezing, not even wanting to breathe. He held his breath for thirty seconds when another shape slid past him, back-dropped by the dark bushes and a moment later Mac smelt the pungent whiff of the second cat and stopped himself from drawing breath, squeezing his chest in growing agony until he judged the leopards to be far enough away to be safe. Quickly he went into his cottage and took the razor-sharp panga off the wall by feeling for it where it hung. Barefoot he went out to follow the leopards that were following the man.

AT FIRST HANK thought one of the gang had slipped an arm around his neck and was trying to make him wrestle but when the pressure on his windpipe increased and choked any sound from his throat, he knew the arm was that of a man and not a boy. A tearing pain shot into his side and then he blacked out from lack of oxygen.

"Hank are you ready?" called back Nteli who had his back to the small fire over which Hank had been testing the mussels to see if they were cooked. Before he turned round, puzzled by Hank's lack of reply, his own windpipe was crushed by the pressure on his Adam's apple and he felt the same searing pain in the side before losing consciousness.

. . .

Away from the shadows of tall grass, Mac was three hundred metres behind the two leopards who were stalking side-by-side. The night sounds were those of waves pushing into shore and dragging back the loose, rounded rocks, a sound like giant shingles rolling. Not even the other members of the gang had noticed anything out of the ordinary when the man-shadow passed Mac on his way back from the rock-ship having circled around the back of it with the leopards following. Kobus Kriel was unaware of anything save the deep, deep pleasure of sweet revenge. He dropped down onto the path and was violently gripped from behind by a hand that clapped silently over his mouth and an arm that held him vice-like across his chest.

"Do you know two leopards are following you?" Mac spoke in Xhosa. "Don't make a sound," and Mac relaxed his hand over the man's mouth and was promptly cursed proficiently in Afrikaans for his troubles, the man breaking away the moment Mac's arm relaxed from his chest.

"He stabbed me," called Hank weakly from the rock having fought his way back to full consciousness, the words reaching Mac over the sound of the sea.

"Aldo Carli." Mac understood. Mac stood perfectly still as the leopards bounded past after their quarry. "You hurt badly?" he called to Hank.

"I'm ok but Nteli's hurt." There was a thud from the path followed by a scream, followed by a growling sound and when Mac three minutes later carried Nteli down the path, his headscarf stuffed firmly into the boy's wound, there was no sign of a body or the leopards; all three had vanished into the night.

. . .

No sooner had the sun pulled itself out of the water then activity burst over the *Bremen*. It was a chase against time and the weather, which *The Great Man* took in his stride, enjoying every moment and by half-past twelve when a fog rolled in from the sea, the picture was in the can.

Hank and his father bought Nteli back from the clinic, both boys impressively swathed in bandages around their waists where Kobus Kriel had tried to stab them through the kidneys but making a mess out of the stabbings as he had done out of everything else in his life. Mac had searched the forest and climbed up the tree next to the hippo fig tree but there was no sign of the dope smuggler or the leopards.

"Wouldn't feel right claiming a reward for a man," he said to himself but he was still puzzled by the lack of any tattered clothing or other signs of the leopards having had themselves a meal. He went back to his cottage and changed for the party trying once more to rub some sense into his arm muscles following the day before's efforts with the cross-cut saw. The pain in his right arm was well worth sixty rand, and he smiled at his own discomfort.

_____

20

*J*ustine dressed to kill. After Mac's slightly intoxicated words spoken in front of the camera, she was convinced he was as dotty about her as she was about him. She could still hear her replies to his spoken love words, what she said to Mac being far more important than the result of her screen test. She had seen him twice during the day but Mac was back to being Mac and there was nothing she could do which would rekindle the looks of passion she had seen in his eyes on the veranda of the long-thatched house.

Mac, favouring his right arm, having admired his new seats outside the restaurant first, was one of the last to arrive and made a good stir dressed in an outfit consisting of a shirt threaded with beads by the local Pondos and a baggy pair of black, silk trousers above large bare feet. He had a new, blood free scarf wrapped around his forehead in a tight roll to keep the long hair out of his way; his beard had been neatly plaited and tied under his chin. A bright Pondo necklace graced his chest, fighting hard with the thick mat of chest hairs. Justine nearly passed out with excitement and shortly afterwards *The Great Man* called for silence and announced that Justine van Heerden was being offered a three-year contract worth three million dollars and even Mac found his mouth shut tight for words. Recovering first, Mac led the clapping. *The Great Man* raised his right hand and silence returned.

"The lady's parents and I agree she must gain her matric before coming to America so her final decision is left until then."

Mac clapped again with the others and padded his bare feet through to the kitchen with Johnny right up behind him.

Fix stopped them on the way. "We picked up Kobus Kriel, alias Aldo Carli. Man was in poor shape. Said they dumped him in the sea and a pair of leopards almost attacked him."

"Who gets the reward?"

"No one. Gave himself up. Said the leopards were still stalking him."

"What will he get?"

"Twenty years for drug smuggling and attempted murder. How are they?"

"Fine. The penknife just cut the flesh. Thanks, Fix."

"My pleasure."

Johnny followed Mac into the kitchen as Fix went off to talk to the Chief of Police. The end-of-film party was well under way.

"Could I have my sixty rand?" asked Mac, giving Hector his best smile. "Hi, Ricky," he grinned but Ricky was unable to look him straight in the face.

"What's going on," said Mac, looking around the kitchen. Outside, Strider was handing Justine a fifty-dollar bill with his phone number written in the top-right corner. Hector handed Mac a piece of paper. On it was written:

One Gander: R10.00
Pain and suffering: R30.00
Unfair competition: R20.00
Total: R60.00

"Makes us even, Mac," said Hector as Johnny burst out laughing. Seeing there was only one thing to do, Mac joined in the laughter as he handed Hank the note.

"Looks like Hector cooked your goose as well," grinned Hank.

∼

The End

ENJOYED THIS BOOK? YOU CAN MAKE A HUGE DIFFERENCE

~

Reviews are the most powerful tools in our kitty when it comes to getting attention for Peter's books. This is where you can come in, as by providing an honest review you will help bring them to the attention of other readers.

If you enjoyed reading *Second Beach,* and have five minutes to spare, we would really appreciate a review (it can be as short as you like). Your help in spreading the word and keeping Peter's work alive is gratefully received.

Please post your review on the retailer site where you purchased this book.

Thank you so much.
Heather Stretch (Peter's daughter)

PS. We look forward to you joining Peter's growing band of avid readers.

PRINCIPAL CHARACTERS

∼

The van Heerdens
Hank — Justine's younger brother
Justine — Hank's elder sister
Mr & Mrs van Heerden — Justine and Hank's parents

The Gang
Nteli — Friend of Hank's and gang leader of 11 other boys

Second Beach Residents
Mac McIntyre — Justine's love interest
Martin — Claims to be a writer and smokes dope all
the time
Johnny — A fisherman
Fix Jalobe — The local magistrate
Hector and Ricky — Owners of the Vuya Restaurant
Aldo Carli — A crook and dope dealer

Film Crew
Strider — A cameraman and later Justine's fiancé
The Great Man — Film Director
Peter Warnaby — Film Producer

GLOSSARY

~

Babalas — Hangover
Bakkie — South African word for pickup truck
Braai — South African barbeque
Matric — South African school-leaving exam
Mealies — Maize/corn
Muti — African word for medicine
Pondo — Xhosa speaking ethnic people who have given
their name to Pondoland in the Eastern Cape